Blink

Tim Laseter

Published by Tim Laseter, 2022.

This is a work of fiction. Names, characters, places, and incidents either are the product of the author's imagination or are used fictitiously, and any resemblance to actual persons, living or dead, businesses, companies, events, or locales is entirely coincidental.

BLINK

First edition. August 26, 2022.

Copyright © 2022 Tim Laseter.

All rights reserved. No part of this book may be reproduced, scanned, or distributed in any printed or electronic form without permission.

Written by Tim Laseter.

For those that answer the call.

BLINK

By
Tim Laseter

It was Mike's turn to drive so Frank had to die. It was as simple as that. Mike and Frank constantly swapped roles between driving the bulky, box ambulance and riding in the back, taking care of the patient. They were never victims; that's what they were before Fort Bend County Emergency Medical Service arrived. Afterward, they were patients, in the care of some of the best paramedics the great state of Texas could certify.

It is strange that such a simple thing – in this case, who is behind the wheel – could lead to an irreversible and unequivocal change in the path of someone's life. Some might call it fate, others, the will of God. Regardless of what you call it, life can change in the blink of an eye.

Mike is young, in his mid-twenties. Thin, clean-shaven, with a full head of dark hair and dark brown eyes. He's been working with the county for seven years now; lucky seven, he calls it. Frank, only ten years older, has been with the county for thirteen years. He is slightly taller than Mike and tends to run a few pounds to the heavy side – a symptom of too many days sitting in the ambulance station waiting for calls. Frank sports a thick mustache and Mike likes to joke it is to make up for his thinning head of blonde hair.

The response is quick; only fifteen minutes from the station to the small, one-story house in the tiny, gated retirement community. The roads are as empty as they can only be at 3 a.m., the red and white lights warning the occasional driver on their way to some unknown place, their vehicles just dark shapes with only the head and tail lights to indicate their presence. As Mike pulls up to the entrance gate he flips the switch to kill the sirens; no sense waking up the entire neighborhood for a medical call where some old lady probably just fell out of bed and couldn't get up, or grandpa needed a blood pressure check because he felt dizzy walking to the bathroom to pee for the fourth time that night.

Mike stops at the curb in front of the red brick house. A single light filters out behind blinds from what is probably the bedroom. After putting the ambulance in park he grabs the mic, hanging on the clip from the dash, and calls dispatch.

"Medic Three on scene," he says, and replaces the mic on its hook.

"Looks like we beat the fire department again," Frank says with a chuckle, "due to your lead foot driving."

"Hey now," Mike replies, "the sooner we put granny back to bed, the sooner *we* can get back to bed."

Mike and Frank step out of the cab simultaneously, and both grab their respective gear from compartments on either side of the ambulance. As Frank's side is closest to the house he walks towards the door first, shouldering the respiratory pack, with Mike right behind him carrying the cardiac monitor and patient clipboard.

The front door is centered on the walkway with large bushes to either side of the small porch. The single overhead light illuminates the wooden front door, which looks in need of a fresh coat of paint. Frank can see the door is slightly ajar, darkness filtering through the crack.

Looking back briefly at Mike, he shrugs his shoulders, faces forward and knocks on the door, which causes it to open further into the dark interior. "Hello, this is ..."

A sudden flash of light drives back the darkness. Then, nothing.

Chapter One

Present Day

The old man that lived there was suffering from dementia," Mike said slowly. He looked up at the faces of the half-dozen men and women seated around him. "He dialed 911 'cause his wife had passed out on the floor. Only, she had died eighteen months prior and he lived alone. He had opened the front door to wait for help. But before we arrived, he began reliving his WW2 days and thought he was under attack by enemy forces. When Frank opened the door, the 9mm round took him directly in the chest. He died within minutes."

A heavy sigh and sob escaped him. "That was almost twenty years ago. I've lived with survivor's guilt ever since, among other things."

Diane, the group counselor for the day, said "Thank you for sharing your story, Mike." Others around the semi-circle nod somberly. "Survivor's guilt is a genuine feeling that people have in situations where others have passed and they somehow survived. It's important to talk about these things and get them out in the open so that, with time, you can begin to heal. I hope you can see that Frank's death was not your fault, and that it happened so quickly that there was no time to do anything to change the outcome."

"Yeah, I know that," Mike said. "It just doesn't help sometimes."

Mike sat quietly and listened to the remainder of the group share their stories, all different but similar in that they all led to this place. A place where people that felt broken came for help. A place to exercise the demons that robbed one's self-esteem and self-worth. The demons that could paralyze you, make you drink and take drugs to forget, yell and scream at the slightest provocation, or get that feeling of crushing tightness in your chest; like you couldn't breathe, like you were having a massive heart attack. You knew deep down inside that you weren't, but it didn't change the sensation in that moment. For Mike, sometimes that sensation was a sudden pain in his chest, just to the left of center, right where the bullet had entered Frank's body.

These support group sessions can help to cope with the post-traumatic stress that comes from witnessing a death. For Mike, who worked for years as a paramedic, death was part of the job. It didn't happen every day, but Old Man Death visited often enough where some medics became numb to it. Mike never did. He always viewed death as a personal failure; after all, the job was to save people. When he could not save someone he essentially felt as if he had failed not only the patient, but the patient's spouse, kids, parents, and friends. That's where the support group came in. It allowed Mike to talk through his different experiences, whichever one was haunting him the most at the moment, and hear from others that shared similar experiences. The group provided support and comfort which let you know you were not alone; that others felt like you did and that it was going to be ok. He didn't attend them as frequently as he used to, but it was good to check in once in a while.

After the counseling session ended, Mike headed to the parking lot. This was the first session in a long time where he had shared that particular story. Out of all the episodes from his days working as a medic, that one was the toughest. Losing a partner suddenly, the investigation that followed, the media attention and ultimately, the change of career. He just hadn't been able to go back to working on the ambulance again. Every time the station tones would sound he'd wondered if this was going to be another bad call; not just for the person calling for help, but for him and his partner.

The county-run service had given him administrative leave with pay for a couple of months to give him a chance to grieve, seek counseling, and get his head straight. It didn't work. Mike felt overwhelming paralysis whenever he tried to go back to work. Ultimately he left the service and became an insurance adjuster.

As Mike settled behind the wheel of his car he caught a glimpse of himself in the rearview mirror. He was in his mid-forties, but the haggard face staring back at him looked older. His dark hair was almost completely gray. *But at least I still have hair*, he thinks. He was sporting a bushy mustache and even that had peppered gray throughout. His cheeks were gaunt and he looked tired. He didn't always sleep well; another symptom of the post-traumatic stress that had haunted him for years.

Mike's foundation, his "rock," that kept him grounded and saw him through the roughest patches was his family – his wife and kid. They stuck by his side and helped him with the bad times. Over the years, the memories faded, the flashbacks became fewer, and Mike began to take back his life. Now, as the twentieth anniversary of that fateful day approached, the flashbacks had returned as vivid as ever.

• • • •

The first had occurred just a few nights ago while eating dinner with his wife Sally.

"How was your day at the office, dear?" she asked, sitting down in front of her salad.

"Same old, same old," Mike replied, digging into his bowl of greens. "Emails, more emails, and I survived another meeting that should have been an email."

"Well, my day was a bit better," she said. "The kids were pretty well behaved today, except for Billy, who almost got into it with another kid on the playground over a ball." She was looking down as she spoke, poking around in her salad bowl, looking for a cherry tomato. "I swear that kid is a magnet for trouble; fortunately, the PE teacher, Ms. Gardner, was able to get over there before things got out of hand." She looked up as she heard a loud clink from the other side of the table.

Mike had dropped his fork, striking the side of the bowl. He sat there, staring off into space, a dazed look in his eyes. Sally had seen this before, but it had been almost non-existent the last few years. "Mike? Honey?" She called softly.

No response. Sally put her fork down and moved over to his side of the table, gently taking his right hand. "It's ok, baby. I'll be right here when you return." She wasn't overly concerned with Mike's "spell," as her momma would have called it. He faded out sometimes when he had flashbacks to his medic days. The doctors said it was part of his PTSD, these flashes. Nothing seemed to trigger them, they just randomly happened and never lasted more than a few seconds. And fortunately, they never happened while he was driving. It's important to reassure him when he returns that he is ok, so she remained quietly by his side, looking down at the back of his hand and rubbing her fingers across its smooth surface.

Mike is riding shotgun today. The siren wails in its low to high frequency voice as they barrel down the freeway, Frank easily passing others in the leftmost lane as drivers move over to make way.

"Exit Highway Six and turn right. The wreck should be about one mile up," Mike says.

Frank exits and easily navigates the intersection, turning right. He has to be a bit more careful now, as traffic can come at him from any direction; side streets, parking lots, or panicked drivers that suddenly slow down at the approach of an emergency vehicle in the rearview mirror.

At each major intersection he slows almost to a crawl, looking to ensure that all other drivers have stopped before proceeding. A wrecked ambulance won't help the victims of the accident they are responding to.

"Medic Three," the dispatcher calls suddenly. Mike grabs the mic: "Go ahead, Medic Three here."

"Medic Three, we have reports of multiple injuries and a possible fatality; dispatching Medic Four to assist."

"Copy," Mike replies. "Put Life Flight on standby." He keeps the mic in hand as they are quickly approaching the accident.

Mike begins his evaluation even before the ambulance rolls to a stop, Frank parking at an angle to the roadway to block the mangled vehicles in front of him.

Looks like a T-bone, *he thinks.* Red Corvette into the drivers' side of the blue Taurus. Significant damage to both. *"Frank, take the Vette, I'll check the Ford," he says out loud.*

Grabbing the trauma kit, Mike heads to the Taurus from the passenger side. Through the rear passenger window he sees a child's car seat in the back, empty. Approaching the front passenger door he sees two occupants, an adult female in the passenger seat and adult male behind the wheel. Blood splatters cover the passenger window but he's able to see movement of the female.

The door is jammed but a good tug gets it open. The lady looks over at him, crying, blood flowing from a gash on the right side of the head. Mike leans in and quickly glances in the back, desperately looking for the kid that may have ejected from the car seat.

"Ma'am," he says, "I'm a paramedic and I'm going to help you. Can you hear me?"

The lady nods weakly.

"Ma'am, where is your child?"

For a moment there is a look of panic in her eyes and she tries to turn around. Mike quickly reaches in and holds her head to restrict the motion in case there is a neck or spinal injury. "Hold still, don't move," Mike commands. His voice is firm, yet gentle. It tells the lady someone has taken charge of the chaos and will help her navigate the next several minutes of her life.

"He's not in the car," she whispers. "At the babysitter."

Thank goodness for small favors, *Mike thinks. Looking over, he sees that the driver is unconscious, but breathing. Normally, he would take priority over an awake, talking person, but Mike can't get to him until she's out of the way. "Just remain still for me," Mike says. "We'll have you out of here shortly."*

Shifting his body so he can semi-stand and look over the top of the car, he catches Frank's eye as Frank steps back from the Corvette. The grim look on his face and curt shake of his head tells Mike all he needs to know.

Grabbing his portable radio off his belt with his free hand, the other still stabilizing the lady's head and neck, he contacts dispatch.

"Medic Three to dispatch, get Life Flight en route for one unconscious adult male with suspected head trauma. Contact PD to advise one fatality," Mike said. In the distance to his left he can hear the sirens of Medic Four approaching, and to his right those of the fire department or police. Good, he thinks, we'll need help with this one.

Suddenly, Mike's eyes open and he's sitting at the dinner table, Sally next to him.

"Sally," he asked, "why are you kneeling next to me?"

"You had a blink," she replied. "Are you ok?"

Mike paused a moment before answering, thinking it through. "Ambulance call, car accident, thought we had a child ejected for a minute there," he said quietly. "How long was I out?"

"The usual," she replied. "Only a few seconds, ten at most."

"Wow," Mike said. "Feels like I was gone for at least twenty minutes. It was so vivid, like I was actually there."

"I'll call Dr. Birachi in the morning," Sally suggested.

Mike shook his head but she was insistent. "Mike, it's been almost a year since your last episode. You need to get checked."

"Look hun," Mike said, "I'm not going to downplay this, but we went through this years ago. There is nothing physically wrong. It's just the PTSD rearing its ugly head again. I'll be fine."

"Well..." she replied, not entirely convinced, "ok, but if the blinks continue you go see your doctor for a checkup. I'm only giving in since you have your upcoming group session; you need to keep that."

"I will. Promise," Mike replied.

· · · ·

Mike started the car engine, and then waved to another member of the support group who was getting into the vehicle parked next to his. Mike's car was an older model Taurus, not unlike the one in the wreck he'd flashbacked to the other night, or blinked, as Sally tended to call it. Most of the time, he was out for only seconds in real time, even though in his head the flashback could last for minutes or even hours. The longest he remembered having once felt like it was a full twenty-four hour shift, although he was only out for five seconds.

Shifting into reverse, he backed up out of the parking spot and headed to the lot exit. The counseling sessions were held every week at six o'clock. He usually only went every few months, but since his blink the other night, Sally had insisted, and he was due for a visit anyway.

Instead of turning left out of the lot and heading home, he turned right onto the roadway. *Time for another visit*, he thought. It had also been a few months since this one.

The cemetery was quiet, but isn't that usually the case?

Mike pulled up and stopped next to the grass lot, killed the engine, and sat for a moment to gather his courage. These visits never got easier, but they were necessary. He owed Frank that much, if not much more.

He stepped out, grabbing the flowers he had picked up on the way over from the counseling session. *One should never visit an old friend like this and not bring flowers.*

It was a short walk to the grave. The late afternoon sun was warm on his neck and sunlight dappled through the trees onto the grass, where Mike spotted a squirrel running. He heard birds chirping nearby. Other than that, he had the whole section of the cemetery to himself.

The headstone was rose-colored granite, with Frank's EMS badge engraved on one side of his name, and the medical caduceus on the other.

"Hi Frank, it's me," Mike said quietly. "I'm sorry I've been away so long this time."

Frank didn't answer.

Mike knelt next to the headstone and placed the flowers down gently. Then he brushed off some leaves that had landed on the base of the stone.

"I can't believe it's been almost twenty years. Sally's good, still working at the school. The kid; man you wouldn't believe how he has grown. Reese is half-way through college, can you believe that? And me? Well, I'm hanging in there, man. I wouldn't have made it without Sal and Reese. They helped me through the rough patches after you died.

"We did some good back in the day didn't we? So many calls... Accidents, falls, heart attacks, seizures; you name it, we did it. But you know, it's not the good calls that I remember, it's the ones that went south, the ones that no matter what we did, it didn't seem to help. Old Man Death had his clutches on some of 'em and wasn't letting go no matter what."

Mike paused as he reflected back. "You know what else? I wouldn't have wanted to do it with anyone else. You always had my back, and I had yours. You were more than just a partner; you were a brother. I guess that's why it still haunts me to this day. I guess that's why *you* still haunt me to this day."

Mike stood up and stretched his back. "Sometimes I have these dreams. Everything is dark around me; the air is stuffy. I'm lying on my back, very still, like I'm in one of those MRI machines. I can feel a silken cloth under my hands, and when I try to raise them, they are blocked by more of that silky cloth. I can't raise my arms more than a few inches before feeling resistance. Then I startle awake. I think I'm dreaming that I'm in that coffin instead of you. Creeps me out every time. My therapist says it is part of the guilt complex I feel for surviving when you didn't."

Mike looked around, startled, as he heard a car door slam. Another visitor coming to pay another loved one their respects. "Listen, man, I need to get going. Busy work week ahead pushing those papers. I'll try not to stay away so long." Mike turned, gently touched the head stone, and headed back to his car.

· · · ·

It was Monday morning and Mike had been at the office for a few hours. The workload was always a bit heavier on Mondays as he had to sift through the stack of new claims from the weekend. His co-worker, Jerry, handled new sales for the firm. He could hear him in the next cubicle on the phone with a potential client, his low voice monotonous as he pitched, trying to close the deal.

He was thinking back to his visit with Frank and feeling distracted. While the upcoming anniversary of the call where Frank died weighed heavily on his mind, that wasn't the only one. He had spoken at Frank's grave about those other calls, the ones where Death had his clutches on his victims and wasn't letting go no matter what. Death, who he sometimes thought of as Old Man Death. Mike envisioned death as this invisible old man, tall and thin, wearing a black suit that was faded and tattered, who robbed people of their souls. When Old Man Death had his clutches in people, sometimes medical professionals were able to pull them from his grasp; other times, his grip, his death grip, was so strong nothing could stop him. It was these calls, where Mike had encountered Old Man Death holding on with the strongest grip, that continued to haunt him.

Mike's flashback episodes, his blinks, had always come without warning, unlike those people who get an aura, sometimes a smell or a weird taste in their mouth that will precede a seizure or panic attack. Mike had never identified a trigger or warning sign; his blinks just seemed to happen out of the blue. Yet, as he sat in his office chair thinking about Frank, thinking about the bad calls, one call in particular begins to wander across his mind. This one involved a kid, and it ended badly. He was thinking about that call, and suddenly...

The Brazos River is wide, deep, and filled with muddy-colored water. It flows gently unless there has been a large rain event. Then, it can rage.

It passes through Medic Three's district for miles; mostly through farmland but also behind master-planned subdivisions, communities that are part of the explosive growth the county has been experiencing in recent years, where it is part of the water runoff plans to prevent flooding in the new million dollar homes. Here, it runs under a major freeway, Highway 59 in the town of Sugar Land, a growing metropolis on the outskirts of Houston. A large bridge traverses the river, and turnaround lanes connect the access roads on both the east and west banks.

It's about one hundred and thirty yards from the edge of the turnaround to the river bank on the east side. Nothing lives here but scrub grass, a few hardy bushes, and the unwanted debris that people have discarded. It has become a dumping ground for old furniture, mattresses, and other detritus that the locals no longer have need for.

Frank has just put the truck in park but Mike had already opened the door and stepped out as soon as the vehicle slowed. They have been called to a possible drowning, and the adrenaline has kicked into high gear.

Up ahead, Mike sees a lady crying hysterically, her presumed husband trying to console her. A Sugar Land police officer is with them, another off in the distance with the fire department crew. No one seems to be moving fast which fills Mike with foreboding. To the right of the fire crew he sees another emergency group unloading a flat-bottomed boat off the back of a trailer. The truck attached to the trailer is emblazoned with the fire department logo, the word Rescue displayed beneath it.

Mike walks up to Tom, the lieutenant of the fire response team. "What do you have, Tom?" he asks.

Tom replies, "Family was down here fishing." He nods towards the man and crying woman. "Ten-year old kid went in the water about 20 minutes ago. The dad tried to find him but couldn't, so he drove to the gas station to call 911." Tom shakes his head, "The clock has been ticking too long for that kid but we called you out in case we need someone to call a time of death."

Mike's heart immediately sinks. "Ok, we'll stand by over here. Let us know if you need anything."

Even though it sounds hopeless, Mike is still hoping for a miracle. The adrenaline has turned to anxiety and a feeling of helplessness. Frank joins him and they move closer to the water's edge. The water is moving at a decent clip. To the left, against one of the concrete pylons that holds up the freeway two-hundred feet above their heads, the bottom of which is buried in the water, there is a large pile of wooden debris; tree limbs and branches from the recent storms that have washed down and collected against the concrete structure. Mike cannot tell how far down it goes, but it sticks above the water by at least six feet and it is a good 20 feet long.

Maybe he's caught up right there, just below the surface, but you would never know it with the muddiness of the water. Can't see anything below the surface. *He wants to help, he wants to just wade in and start feeling around, but he knows how dangerous that would be. Mike is not trained in water rescue; that's the fire crew's role. His role is to wait.*

The minutes feel like hours as Frank and Mike watch the rescue team in the boat. They have the outboard motor running to keep the boat from drifting downstream, and are using poles to probe the water. They are about 15 feet in front of the visible edge of the wood pile.

The mom continues to sob, but it's quieter now as exhaustion sets in.

The agonizing waiting continues. The only sounds are the hum of the outboard motor and the thump thump as cars overhead pass over the bridge's concrete seams. They both stand there, the emergency airway bag, trauma kit, and cardiac monitor surrounding their boots.

Frank turns to Mike. "It's been 45 minutes, let's get the unit back in service." Mike can tell he is upset, but Frank is also a realist. "Kid's dead. Nothing we can do here."

Resigned, Mike nods and picks up the cardiac monitor and airway bag.

They turn and begin the march back to the truck.

Suddenly they hear a disturbance behind them. The lady is wailing louder now. Turning, they see the rescue team on the shore with the lifeless kid. They immediately head down to do their required duty.

First instinct is to work the kid. Start cardiopulmonary resuscitation, get an IV going, and rush the kid to the nearest emergency room. But reality is the kid was dead after five to six minutes in the water without oxygen. Working the kid will only give the parents false hope, take the unit out of service when it might be needed for a patient that can be saved, put others at risk with an emergency run to the hospital, and leave the parents with a pile of medical bills. They have enough to manage without all that.

The kid is on his back with his head turned to the side. Ashen, pale, lifeless. Even though the situation is hopeless, Mike's training kicks in.

The litany of evaluating a patient. First, check the airway to ensure it is open. Then listen and look for any signs of breathing. Finally, feel for a pulse. Mike does all of this automatically. Airway is open, no signs of respirations, no pulse, *he thinks. While he is doing this, Frank pulls the cardiac leads – the thin wires that will detect any electrical activity of the heart – out of the zippered pouch on the side of the monitor, attaches the sticky pads to the far end of them, and plugs the wires into the monitor. Mike reaches down and lifts the sopping wet t-shirt and applies the cardiac monitor pads, one each to the upper left and right of the chest, and the third on the lower left side of the body. As he does this he sees water and white foam pouring out of the kid's mouth. His stomach does a flop.*

Frank then turns on the Lifepak 10 cardiac monitor and both glance at the small display screen to check for any heart activity. Flat line. Frank presses the record button which will run a paper strip, similar to a receipt paper you get at a retail store, of the lack of heart activity. The monitor spits out the paper for six seconds, then stops. Frank tears off the paper, which shows a flat line down the middle, as well as the date and time the recording was made, and puts it in his uniform shirt pocket.

"OK, that's it," Mike says, removing the leads. "I'll radio the Medical Director from the truck."

He picks up the equipment, trying to still his shaking hands. This kid is so young. I can't imagine what the parents must be going through.

As Mike walks away, he knows he will never get the picture of that kid out of his head, nor that sound of the wailing mom. He feels helpless, worthless, completely and utterly wracked with guilt for not being able to do anything. For just standing there and waiting for others to find the kid. He should have done something. He should have gone in the water and checked the wood pile. Mike doesn't care that too much time had gone by before they arrived, he could have at least tried; shown the parents that he was doing *something, trying anything to help find their little boy.*

"Mike?" Frank calls. He sees Mike veering off, not heading towards the truck anymore. He looks very distressed, almost angry. He's never seen

Mike look that way before.

Mike spots a debris pile just off the roadway in the dirt. An old desk, some filing cabinets, and some wooden plywood that's partially rotted. He heads towards it, the feeling of helplessness driving him to take action, to do something. His body fills with rage and anger. He's never felt like this after a call but this one has just gotten to him.

He drops the kits to the ground as he reaches the pile of debris, and pulls back his right arm, making a fist and throwing a punch with all he's got at the plywood, propped up against the old desk. The wood makes a cracking and thumping sound as his fist strikes it. Mike is not used to hitting things, and the pain in his hand is immediate and intense, but also welcome, as it takes his mind off of the kid. He hits it again, and again, now he's hitting it with both fists and screaming.

Frank is at his shoulder, trying to get him to stop. Mike can hear him yelling behind him.

Suddenly, his right fist breaks through the rotted plywood. The jagged wooden edge opens a large, wicked laceration on the back of his hand. That breaks the spell of rage and anger.

"Shit!" Mike cries out, shaking his hand, blood flying on the boards and his uniform. He clutches his bleeding hand with his other one, trying to stop the bleeding. "Damn it!"

Frank is there with him. "Hold on, let me get some gauze on that before you bleed to death!" he commands.

Within minutes Frank has the wound dressed. Mike is sitting on the edge of the desk, slowly calming down.

"I'm sorry, Frank. I don't know what came over me. You know I'm not like this. It's just…that kid…he shouldn't have died today. He was only ten! Hell, that could have been my kid!"

Frank replies gently, "Well, you are right in that he shouldn't have died today. But it wouldn't be your kid. First off, your kid is still a toddler and second, I know you will never let him out of your sight, especially around water."

Mike nods. "You're right about that." A pause. "I'm going to need stitches. Plus I need to call our supervisor; he won't be pleased."

Frank thinks for a moment before answering. "Ok, here's what happened. You fell. Tripped on the debris and cut your hand. You say anything else and you will most likely end up suspended. The others are too far away and didn't see what happened; it was too fast. I'll back you up on this, got it?"

"OK, Frank," Mike replies. "I owe you one."

"... so then we saw that new Bond movie that just came out and went to dinner. It was a good first date," Jerry finished. "Hey, did you hear me?" he popped his head over the cubicle wall.

Mike was sitting still, staring at the computer screen. It had only been a moment, just long enough for Jerry to tell him about his blind date and wonder at the lack of witty one liners from Mike.

Mike blinked his eyes and looked up. "What? I'm sorry, I must have spaced out for a second there."

He glanced down at his hands on the computer keyboard. An ugly, pale scar ran the length of his right hand, traversing from the base of his thumb to his ring finger. *What the heck?* he thought. *That was NOT there before.*

"Mike, you ok?" Jerry asked, a look of concern on his face.

"Yeah, yeah, right as rain," Mike replied, still staring at his hand. He ran his left index finger across the scar. Looked old; no pain.

"Hey Jer, did I ever tell you the story about this scar?" Mike asked.

Jerry leaned over the wall farther to see what Mike's talking about. "That? Yeah, something about falling when you were working on the ambulance a hundred years ago," he replied with a grin. "You always are kinda clumsy," he said.

"Yep. I guess I am," Mike replied.

· · · ·

Later that night, Mike was home with Sally at the dinner table. Sally noticed that Mike was quieter than usual.

"Hun, you have been pushing your food around the plate and not eating. What's bothering you?" she asked.

Mike paused before answering, not sure where to start. He had spent most of the afternoon with his mind half on work, half on the problem of the scar. He remembered the Brazos drowning vividly. It was one of those calls that stuck with him throughout the years. Hanging out at the station with Frank, getting the alert tones, racing to the Brazos turnaround, the waiting, the helpless waiting. What he didn't remember was the scar. He hadn't gotten angry and thrown punches at a pile of junk. He was not that kind of guy. Mike had always dealt with the calls in other ways, usually in silence; not the most healthy way to deal with it, but that was the job. You did the job and you went home alive to your family. That's how you got through it. And if you didn't have family, sometimes you drank or did drugs, or coped in other ways. But Mike had family, and he went to the station every shift with one goal in mind – to get home to his family at the end of the shift. To his wife and little boy. But the scar was new...he was sure that never happened. As he looked down at his hand it glared back at him, like a wicked grin from some alien monster.

"Sal," he said, "did I ever tell you how I got this scar?"

Sally glanced over her glass of wine as she took a sip. "Oh, that old thing? Of course you did. That was an ugly one, as I remember. You had around ten stitches and had to take a week off to let it heal. Why?"

"But how did it happen?" Mike asked.

"Well, that was a long time ago, but something about falling and catching it on some junk. I don't remember any more than that, hun."

"Do you remember when it happened?"

"It was while you were still working on the ambulance. Why? Is it bothering you? Are you in pain from it?" she asked with a note of concern in her voice.

"No. Not painful. Just curious is all." He wasn't sure how to tell her what he was thinking without sounding crazy. He knew without a doubt that the scar hadn't been there until today, when he'd had a blink episode at work. But both Jerry and Sally said it had been there for years. How could that be? How could the flashback he experienced have suddenly changed? Did his recollection of the events change? Had he forgotten about the event that caused the scar? Or had he, somehow, altered the event in the past leading to a decades-old scar he could see and touch, but had no recollection of outside of the recent flashback? And if he *had* somehow changed a past event, could he do it again?

Chapter Three

John Cray wasn't thinking about consequences; he wasn't considering how the smallest of actions could lead to a devastating, life-altering moment in time. He was thinking about protecting his family and property. After all, that was why he had purchased the Remington shotgun. Just point and pull the trigger; no aiming other than in the general direction of the home invader would do.

A recent series of local news stories about home invasions were what prompted the purchase. In some cases, the bad guys would follow a vehicle into the neighborhood and then attack the owner when he pulled into his garage, catching him or her unaware. Other, just as bold, criminals would kick in the front door, surprising the family over dinner or their evening television show. Fortunately no one had been killed yet, but several home owners had been pistol-whipped by mask-wearing robbers, and all had been terrorized in their own homes.

So John Cray purchased the shotgun.

He kept it in the small, narrow laundry room adjacent to the garage; no one would follow *him* home to surprise him with an assault and robbery. He kept a good lookout in his rearview mirror. Sometimes he would drive around the neighborhood if a car was behind him just to be sure he was not being followed. Some people might call that being paranoid but Cray called it being careful. However, should someone make it into his garage before the door closed, he would fall back into the laundry room, where the bad guys would get a nasty surprise.

Cray was careful with the weapon. He kept it up on a long shelf above the washer, out of reach of his young children. As they got older, he knew he would need to find a better way to secure it, but for now it was up high and they didn't even know it was there. He kept it loaded with the safety off in case it was needed in a hurry.

He had only owned it for a few weeks and liked to take it down off the shelf to look at it and wipe it down. John liked to keep the dust off;

a clean weapon is a working weapon, as his drill sergeant used to say. He would admire the intricate scrollwork on the side of the large barrel as he gently wiped it clean, and would use a little gun oil to keep the metal surfaces glistening, although that tended to make it a bit slippery.

Those were all the small decisions, perhaps inconsequential by themselves, that altered Cray's path of life. The decision to purchase the shotgun, to keep it up on a high shelf, to keep a round in the chamber, to keep the safety off, to oil it frequently, and yes, the split-second decision to get out of his favorite armchair one afternoon and go take another peek at his new "toy." If any one of these small decisions had been decided differently it would have broken the chain of events that led to the unintended results. Only one change was needed. However, for John Cray, the links in the chain were all connected, and the chain was about to be wielded by Old Man Death himself.

John reached up to grab the shotgun. It was on the shelf above his head, so he had to flex up onto the balls of his feet to reach it. The washroom was narrow, and he was a big guy, so he flexed up, using one hand to steady himself on the washing machine, the other hand blindly reaching up for the gun.

He felt the cold, hard steel of the barrel. The last, fatal omission that John made was to not adjust his grip down towards the stock of the gun, so that the weight would be more evenly balanced. He grasped the barrel, not realizing he was more than halfway down the length of it. As he slid it off the shelf, his other hand still balancing against the washer, the weight of the stock caused the shotgun to drop suddenly. The latest coating of gun oil on the barrel prevented him from gripping it tighter, and further exacerbated his tenuous hold on the weapon. It quickly went from a horizontal position to a vertical one, the barrel facing upwards towards the ceiling.

John attempted to pull the weapon towards him to prevent it from striking the hard surface of the washing machine, and by doing so, pointed the business end of the barrel at the underside of his chin.

The stock of the gun struck the washing machine top, hard. Very hard.

Inside the weapon, the firing pin shifted. Only slightly, but enough to strike the back of the round in the chamber. The striking of the round resulted in the discharge of the gun, sending the round through the bottom of John Cray's jaw and upwards into his head. The force of the blast, in addition to taking off the upper back portion of his skull, caused him to fall backwards onto the tile floor, the gun coming to rest across his twitching legs.

One of the worst calls to roll on; a shooting. So many unknowns. Are there hostiles? How many people are injured? Is the weapon, or weapons, secured? Is the scene safe to enter? This last question gets answered by the police officers responding. For responding fire and EMS crews the initial task is to get close, then wait for the police to enter and tell you it is safe.

Mike and Frank have just been cleared to make the scene. They have staged a block away with a fire department first responder truck immediately behind them.

Parking in front of the home, they both enter through the garage, which is open. A policeman exits the garage holding a shotgun in his gloved hand. "He's just inside there," he says, pointing to the interior house door in the garage.

Mike and Frank quickly enter followed by three firemen.

They find John Cray face up on the floor. His blood is splattered on the wall across from the washing machine, along with some small, grayish bits that can only be one thing. A pool of blood is under his head and torso, and his neck is all but invisible under the glistening red.

Mike steps through the blood to get to John's head. Kneeling, he quickly checks for respirations and a pulse. The breathing is shallow and rapid. Placing his fingers gently against the patient's neck, he feels a fast carotid pulse. Given what he observed on the wall, Mike's surprised to find both, but it happens. The brain damage is most likely severe and not survivable, but if the bullet misses the section of the brain that manages vital functions, the heart continues to beat and the lungs continue to feed the body oxygen.

"Ok," Mike says, "we got an entry wound under the chin, exit out of the top of the head. Still breathing with a pulse." He looks up at the firemen. "Grab a backboard and stretcher. Set up two IV's of Lactose Ringers in the back of the box. We are going to move him as soon as I secure the airway."

Frank immediately moves to the side of the torso in the narrow space and reaches out to hold the head still, securing the spinal column until a neck brace can be applied.

Mike has opened up the airway kit. Grabbing the laryngoscope and Macintosh blade, he quickly assembles it by sliding the blade onto the scope handle, flips it open to check the light, and grabs a size seven airway tube. The blade is not a blade in the sense of a knife blade, but a curved metal form that is used for moving the tongue out of the way so the breathing tube can be inserted into the trachea, the opening leading to the lungs.

Normally, he would need to tilt the head back to fully open the airway for the intubation, placing a breathing tube in so that the patient can be ventilated with oxygen, but with the possibility of a neck injury, either from the bullet or from the fall to the ground, Mike must perform the intubation without moving the head or neck.

He kneels down further, his body and head positioned at the top of the patient. Leaning in, he can hear the rasping breathing as John's body fights to stay alive. He can smell the blood; coppery and metallic in the air. Mike can also feel a cool dampness under his right knee; that can only be one thing soaking through his uniform pants, but in the small space he has to work, there is no way to avoid kneeling in the increasing circle of blood around the patient's head and shoulders.

Gently sliding the laryngoscope blade into the patient's mouth, he lifts the handle upwards, shifting up the lower jaw and lifting the tongue to reveal the two holes, one leading to the lungs, the other to the stomach. Blood is filling the mouth, bubbling in the back of the throat as the patient attempts to breathe. The blood bubbles pop, spraying small crimson droplets into the air and back onto the patient's lips.

Mike sees the trachea at the end of the lighted instrument and slips the breathing tube in. He quickly removes and drops the scope, and using the air syringe attached to the tube, inflates the small balloon at the far end of it which will hold the tube in place in the airway. Now the breathing sound is coming from the end of the tube instead of the man's mouth.

Grabbing the Bag-Valve-Mask, or BVM, Mike attaches it to the breathing tube with one hand while holding the tube against the patient's lips with the other. They must check to make sure the tube is correctly placed, even though he can hear the breathing through the end of it. A tube that ends up in the esophagus will pump air into the stomach instead of the lungs, depriving the patient of life-saving oxygen.

Frank, holding the head with one hand, grapples with and gets his stethoscope into his ears, and places the diaphragm end of it against the patient's chest. He listens as Mike squeezes the BVM. Nodding the affirmative, he moves the stethoscope to two other places to check for breath sounds, then over the upper middle abdomen to ensure he does not hear sounds in the stomach. "You're in, Mike," he says.

Mike uses a crisscross pattern with the first aid tape to secure the tube in place. He quickly connects the oxygen tank to the BVM with a clear tube, then places both hands on the BVM and, every time the patient takes a shallow breath, he gives it a squeeze to further inflate the man's lungs.

By this time, the fire team has returned with the needed equipment. Things move quickly from here with Mike directing the team. The cervical collar is placed first to further secure the neck. John is rolled to the left side so the long, wooden backboard can be placed under him. Rolling him back onto the board, he is secured to it using a nylon webbing material, criss-crossed from shoulders across his body several times, and tied off at the bottom of the board near his feet.

The board is lifted on the stretcher and is in the back of the ambulance in less than 10 minutes. The IV bags are prepped and ready to go, dangling from hooks embedded in the ceiling of the compartment.

As one of the firemen obtains a blood pressure reading – "90 over 50," he calls out, "pulse, 120 and weak" – Mike inserts a large bore IV needle into the man's left arm, at the crook of the elbow. Another fireman has taken over the duty of assisting with respirations. Based on the vital sign readings and evident loss of blood, Mike opens up the control knob on the IV to flood the patient with the life-saving liquid. It doesn't replace the lost blood completely, as it cannot carry oxygen, but it will replace the blood volume and stabilize the blood pressure and heart rate until they reach the local trauma center.

Mike quickly starts the second IV as Frank readies the ambulance to move out. With the airway and IV's in place, and as the ambulance begins to roll, Mike grabs some sterile dressings to place over the entry and exit wounds, being ever so gentle to ensure he doesn't press on any of the broken skull fragments.

Based on the mechanism of injury being a shotgun blast to the head, brain matter on the wall, and an exit wound out the back of the head, Mike is pretty confident that this guy is not going to make it. But his job is to try to deliver him alive to the emergency room of the local trauma center. If he can do that, maybe the patient can be an organ donor, and help several other ill or injured people. If that can happen, his death won't be a total loss – although that's probably a small consolation to the man's family.

Mike reaches over to check the blood pressure and...

.... opened his eyes to find himself staring back in the bathroom mirror. His eyes were haggard, dark circles under each. Looking over at the bathroom clock, he saw it was three a.m. He decided to head to the kitchen and put on a pot of coffee. He didn't think he would go back to sleep that night.

· · · ·

Sally opened her eyes as Mike slowly walked past the bed and out the door but remained motionless, not wanting to disturb him.

She was becoming increasingly worried about him. He looked tired all the time, and this was the fourth time she had woken to find him in the bathroom just staring at the vanity mirror.

After 35 years of marriage, she knew that look; the blank stare, the slackening of the jaw. The blinks usually didn't last long, hence the term that she penned years ago as a family nickname for Mike's episodes. It was easier to explain to the kid that way. "Daddy's having a blink," she would say, "just give him a moment and he'll be ok." That usually reassured Reese that everything was fine, especially since Mike generally came out of the flashbacks peacefully. Only occasionally would he startle back to reality, a sudden jerk or flailing of arms; those were the really bad calls being remembered, like the one where Frank died.

They are increasing in frequency, Sally thought. *I don't know why, unless it's the upcoming anniversary of Frank's death. But that was so long ago. I was hoping the guilt and memories would fade into the background and give Mike some peace of mind.*

Rolling over in bed, she faced the window that looked out over their backyard. *Should I call Dr. Birachi?* she wondered. *Or just let him work through it?*

Dr. Birachi had been Mike's psychiatrist and therapist for the past fifteen years, although he hadn't needed much more than an annual check for the past few years as the blinks had been few and far between. They'd tried a variety of different treatment modalities including psychotherapy, group sessions, individual sessions, and medications (Mike didn't like the meds, made him feel fuzzy in the head, he would say). None of those by themselves did the trick, but the group sessions seemed to help the most. Probably because he was surrounded by others with similar PTSD problems, although the causes were different. Some were even the result of the very same traumatic experiences that Mike had dealt with as a medic, but they were the victims, patients, or family members of those situations; the victims of a senseless death from a stabbing, beating, or car accident. They were those that wondered why they had survived and others just one seat over did not. They were people that were struggling with why God would have allowed such a tragic event to occur to them or their loved one, why fate had dealt them such a horrible blow.

The group sessions helped, but they were not a cure. There was no cure for the post-traumatic stress Mike had. It was all about learning to live with it and not drive yourself crazy, or drive those around you away.

Sally decided she would talk to Mike about calling the therapist. If she called without him knowing it would just add to his stress level. If Mike decided to make the call, that gave him some level of control over the situation. She would talk to Reese first though, and get his take on the situation. It was time to check in with their son anyway.

· · · ·

Dude, you don't look good," Jerry commented the next morning at the office.

"Mmff," Mike replied, taking a sip of hot coffee as he headed out of the break room. "Not sleeping well lately."

"Want to talk about it?" Jerry asked softly.

He'd worked with Mike a long time and knew his background, how he used to be a paramedic and how he gave it up and eventually ended up working in the insurance industry. Mike had talked about some of the calls with him but not the really bad ones, and Jerry knew better than to ask. Some people will ask a medic, "What's the worst thing you have ever seen," but Jerry knew that that was a horrible question to ask a medic, or a nurse or doctor for that matter. It's akin to asking them to relive some of the most stressful and difficult moments of their life. If they want to talk about it you listen, but it has to be on their terms.

Jerry liked to think of Mike as more than a co-worker. They'd gone out for beers a few times. It was hard to get Mike to open up, but Jerry thought that was, in part, due to the fact that they worked together. It can be hard to trust someone in the office to not spread gossip or rumors. Jerry wasn't that way, and he hoped Mike realized that. The other part was that it was probably just too hard for him to open up after years of having to bottle up his emotions when dealing with some of the worst moments in people's lives. As a paramedic, Mike must have had to suppress emotions when dealing with the pain and suffering that came with the job, making it difficult to bring emotions back to the surface and bare them for anyone to see.

"Nah, I'm good. Really," Mike said with a small smile. "Just working through some stuff is all."

"Ok," Jerry replied. "But if you need to go grab a cold one and talk, I'm here for you, man."

"Thanks, Jerry. I appreciate that."

Chapter Four

Reese had just stepped back into his dorm room when his phone rang. Grabbing the phone from his hip pocket he looked down at Mom's picture smiling at him. Of course, he already knew it was her from the pleasant, jazzy ringtone he had assigned to her.

"Hi Mom. How's it going?" he said, walking over to drop his backpack on the desk.

"Good honey, it's good. How about you? Everything going ok at school?" she asked.

Reese was in his sophomore year at college. It was an adjustment being away from his parents as he was very close to them and, unlike some of his college friends, actually enjoyed his family time. The school was only a few hours' drive away, though, so he went home once every couple of months when the workload wasn't too heavy to hang out and play board games with his folks.

"Yea, it's all good. Classes haven't been too hard this semester, although Modern History is kicking my butt. I can't understand why that class is part of my technology curriculum; probably because no one would take it otherwise," he said. "Is Dad ok?"

"Well, that's actually why I called you," she said, then was quick to add, "He's ok, no heart attacks or anything." A brief pause, and then: "His blinks are back. He's had more this past week than in the past year. I can tell it's bothering him and I'm not sure if I should call the doctor or not. Sometimes he just needs to work through it, you know? But I would like your opinion. What do you think?"

Reese was too young to remember his dad's time in EMS. He'd seen photographs in the family album of himself up at the ambulance station with his dad, sitting in the front cab of the ambulance, as well as some pictures of Dad with his partners over the years, especially Frank. He was with Frank, his last partner, the longest, so naturally there were more pictures of them together.

Reese *does* remember growing up with his father's PTSD. Those times when he would become distant, sometimes irritable, although he never took it out on Reese or Mom. Reese would wake up at night to go pee and find Dad sitting in the living room, just staring at the blank TV screen. He would ask him if he was ok, and Dad would sometimes startle and look surprised, as if not sure where he was at, but he would always recognize Reese when he spotted him at the edge of the living room. He would smile his dad-smile and nod. "Yea kid, I'm good. Go back to bed," he would say softly. And Reese would do just that, usually forgetting the encounter by the next morning, as sleepy kids do.

"Well, Mom," Reese started, "you should probably talk to him first. I mean, he has dealt with the blinks for most of his adult life. He is usually able to work it out. Anything unusual this time or anything making you more concerned, other than the increase?"

"He had an episode at the dinner table the other night. It was short, like they usually are. But when he came out of it he seemed bothered by that old scar on the back of his hand. He looked at it like he had never seen it before; it was pretty strange. He said it wasn't bothering him, but I could tell something was wrong. Normally he comes out of the blinks and needs some quiet time to reflect and process it, but I've never seen that look before," she said.

"Listen," Reese replied, "I have a pretty light class load next week, no tests or papers due. How about I run home for a quick visit this weekend? I would love to catch up and play a few games with you both and it would give me a chance to talk to him if the blinks don't settle back down to a normal level this week. What do you say?"

Sally gave a sigh, almost of relief; she had wanted to ask him to come home, but hadn't wanted to interfere with his school work. It was easy to get behind with that sort of thing. "That would be great, hun. I'd like that and I know your dad would love to see you."

"Ok, done deal," Reese said easily. "I'll see you on Saturday about mid-day then. Love you, Mom. Everything will be ok."

"Thanks. See you this weekend. Love you back."

Sally disconnected the call. It would be great to have Reese home for a couple days. And he had developed a great adult relationship with his father so he'd be able to talk to him about things if needed.

She felt a little better but still had that nagging feeling that things were not quite right with Mike. That something with the blinks had changed, and not in a good way.

. . . .

Mike pulled up in front of the building and shut off the engine. He had cut out of work an hour early, telling his supervisor he had an appointment. It wasn't a lie, not really. He did have an appointment, just not the type that his supervisor probably imagined.

It had been years since he'd stopped by EMS headquarters. The last time was about five years ago for the reunion. The new building was twice the size as the original; to the right were the vehicle bays, doors open, the front of the ambulances pointing outward for a fast response. There were three units parked there, demonstrating the growth of the area since Mike left the service. When he worked for the county, there was only one unit stationed at headquarters and the area felt more rural; now, this region of the county felt like a medium-sized city.

He entered the building on the left of the truck bays through the main door. The Fort Bend EMS logo was emblazoned on a beautiful metal sign above the door. Inside, there was a small waiting room with a counter dividing about a quarter of it into office space for the receptionist. Through a glass window behind the receptionist he could see the dispatch area, currently staffed with three emergency workers, but with room for up to six; another indication of the growth the county had experienced. With more people comes a higher volume of wrecks, heart attacks, and violence.

"Can I help you?" the young receptionist asked. She looked to be about twenty; dressed sharply in her light blue EMS uniform. The

EMT patch was proudly displayed on her right shoulder, and her silver name tag on the front of the shirt read 'Smith.'

"Hello, Ms. Smith," Mike said with a friendly smile. "I'm here for an appointment with the director."

"Please have a seat. I'll let him know you are here," she replied, with a friendly smile of her own.

A few minutes later, Director Stevens entered. He was tall, about six foot four, and thin, with sandy brown hair graying at the temples. He gave Mike a big grin under his bushy mustache, also peppered with gray. "Mike! Good to see you!" he exclaimed.

Mike stood and they briefly shook hands, which quickly turned into an embrace prompted by Stevens.

"Good to see you, too, Chuck," Mike replied.

"Come on back to the office. Can I get you anything? Water? Coffee?" Chuck asked.

"A coffee would be great, thanks," Mike said.

Stevens led Mike through a door into a long hallway, where they walked a short distance and turned left into the kitchen area – part break room for the office staff, and fully equipped kitchen area for the crews that spend twenty-four hours on duty here.

"Black?" Chuck asked.

"Yeah, please."

As Chuck got the Keurig going he asked, "How are Sally and Reese?"

"All good. Sally's still at the school. Reese is in his second year of college," Mike answered. "Congrats on making Director. Well deserved."

"Thank you," Chuck replied. "I guess I drew the short straw," he said with a chuckle.

"Come on," Mike said with a chuckle of his own. "Can't be all that bad. Cushy office with a view. No longer having to pull folks out of wrecked cars on the side of the highway."

"Yeah, I replaced that with budgets and dealing with the county politicians," Chuck replied with a grin. "But it's not too bad for all that."

They headed back down the hallway to Stevens' office, which was indeed cushy, with a leather sofa at one end, an attached conference area for meetings, and a large, oak desk with two arm chairs in front of it. A large window behind the desk looked out over a grassy field and in the distance, a wooded area. Another window on the opposite wall looked into the dispatch area, allowing the Director to see the electronic board showing the status of all fifteen units he oversees.

"So," Chuck said, "what brings you by? What can I help you with?"

"Well, first off, thanks for seeing me on such short notice," Mike said. "I know you are a busy man. The thing is, I've been thinking about this call I was on...with Frank. It was this kid that drowned in the Brazos..." He fades off.

"That's the call where you got that cut on your hand, right? When you beat up that pile of junk," Chuck said.

"You know about that?" Mike said. "Did Frank..."

Chuck cuts him off, "No, Frank didn't give you up. One of the fire guys was back at the truck loading up equipment and saw you. He reported it out of concern."

"I can't believe you remember that," Mike said, with wonder in his voice.

"Mike, I was your shift supervisor. Part of my job was to keep an eye on my crews, and some of the more memorable stuff sticks around up here," he said, tapping his temple.

"But you never said anything about it."

"I kept an eye out for you, Mike. You needed to blow off some steam and you did. I didn't see any repeats so I closed the file on it."

"Thanks for that," Mike said. "You were always my favorite supervisor, you know."

"Yea, yea, I bet you said that to all the shift supervisors," Stevens said with a laugh.

"So this kid," Mike said again, "I can't get him out of my head at times. It's one of the calls that just sticks with me." He tapped his head like Chuck had done a moment before. "But I can't remember his name for the life of me. I know it probably breaks all kinds of privacy rules nowadays, but could you look up the call and tell me his name? I'd like to go pay my respects, you know? It's one of those calls that I feel like I failed and it might help bring me some closure."

Chuck Stevens looked across the desk at Mike, an empathetic look on his face. He got it. He had some of those demons as well. The calls that didn't go well, the ones where you were simply too late, or the person was too damaged to save. "You are right, it does break some rules." A pause, then, "But I have executive privilege and get to say when those rules can be bent a little. You know, though, you will need more than a name to find this kid's final resting spot. I'm happy to help, but this can't come back to me, got it?"

"Agreed. And thanks again," Mike replied gratefully.

"Lucky for you, we digitized all the old records a few years back. That helps us with trending our statistics all the way back to the early days of the department." Chuck began tapping on his computer keyboard. "Do you remember what year that was? It will help me narrow down the search."

Mike did remember. "It was in '94. Summer. June, I think."

More typing on the keyboard.

"Ok, we had five drownings that month according to the summary stat page. Let me drill down into this."

More typing on the keyboard. Chuck leaned towards the screen. "Ok, got it. Drowning, Highway 59 at Brazos River turnaround, June 5th, 1994. Kid's name was Joe Valdez, mom is Juanita, dad is Juan. DOB is August 11, 1983... Just a few months shy of his eleventh birthday. Parents' address at the time was 1511 Avenue H in Stafford. You want me to write this down for you?"

"Ahead of you," Mike replied. He had reached over while Chuck was reading and grabbed a post-it note pad and pen off of his desk. "I should be able to research and find the cemetery with this. I really appreciate it, Chuck," Mike said, rising and extending his hand.

"Hey, glad I can help. And I hope this helps quiet the demons for a while." Chuck reached out and shook Mike's hand. "It's good to see you again. Don't stay away so long next time. We've missed you."

Chapter Five

S tafford was another of those small towns on the outskirts of Houston. Landlocked between Houston, Missouri City and Sugar Land, it hadn't seen the population growth of those larger cities. It was an older town that still had that old feel; a workers' town. Its geographical location made it part of Medic Four's district back in the day, although Medic Three would frequently back them up on calls.

The house on Avenue H had seen better days. A small, single-story home, it was surrounded by a rusty chain link fence. The yard was bare down to the dirt throughout. The yellow paint had faded and was peeling in several places; it looked like it hadn't seen the business end of a paint brush in at least two decades. The two windows, flanking the metal screen door, were covered in tin foil on top, both with a small air conditioning unit sticking out the bottom half like angry tongues sticking out at the world. A beat up Ford truck sat in the driveway, the rear passenger wheel up on a jack stand, the tire missing.

Mike sat in his car across the street from the old house. He wasn't sure if the Valdez family still lived there or not. He wasn't sure if he should go see. In fact, he wasn't sure of much of anything at the moment. He'd told Director Stevens that this wouldn't come back to him, but if he went to the door and things went wrong, they were going to demand to know how he'd found them. He'd never give up Chuck, but he needed a good cover story first.

If they did still live there, did he want to lie to them? Mike wasn't not a liar; he always told it straight. So maybe "honesty would be the best policy" as his dad used to say. Or at least a form of it. Maybe he had found them online while researching Joe's final resting place. He had found a couple articles on the drowning, one about the incident itself and the other with the funeral arrangements – a viewing at the funeral home followed by the burial. That was all true. He could just leave out what had put him on the trail in the first place.

What could he even say after so many years? 'I'm thinking of your dead kid who I couldn't save. Feeling a bit guilty and looking for some solace and peace.' Yeah, that would go over like a brick dropped from a second-story window. Would it bring up memories that, even now, were too painful for the parents to be reminded of? After all, no parent should have to bury their child. You don't heal from that, not fully. Would knowing that Mike still thought of him, that he kept his memory of this boy he never knew alive, help or hurt them?

Mike sighed and reached for the gear shift. *I don't think I can do this*, he thought.

Suddenly the front door to the house opened. A woman stepped out onto the stoop, staring at Mike's car. She couldn't have seen him there, not with the foil on the windows, but now that she had stepped out, she'd definitely noticed him.

She was Hispanic and looked to be about the right age, in her mid-fifties. She was dressed in faded denim and a loose t-shirt. Her right hand held a plastic bag, her left, what appeared to be a beer bottle. She shuffled slowly down the steps then veered left, headed for the trash bins placed just off the concrete path. She stopped and glanced suspiciously at the blue car parked across the street.

Mike paused in his effort to put the car in gear. *It's her*, he thought. *It's the mom. Older, haggard, but her nonetheless.*

Making up his mind, Mike left the car in park and shut off the engine. Stepping out into the street, he gave a small wave and smiled at the woman, who was still eyeing him warily as she placed first the trash bag in one bin, and then the beer bottle in another.

"Hi," Mike called, slowly walking across the road towards the fence.

Still suspicious, she turned to face him but didn't approach any closer. "Can I help you?" she asked.

"Are you Juanita?" Mike replied, stopping on the sidewalk. "Juanita Valdez?"

"Do I know you?"

Mike hesitated for just a moment. *Now or never.* "No. No you don't. I was one of the medics that was there...that day. The day that Joe..." He couldn't bring himself to finish the sentence. Mike grasped one hand in the other in front of his body, absentmindedly rubbing the scar on the back of his hand. Suddenly he was filled with emotions, tears springing to his eyes.

The woman nodded slowly. "Yes, I'm Joey's mom, Juanita," she replied, now approaching the fence. "You were there?"

Mike cleared his throat. "Um, yea. I was. I just wanted to....to say how sorry I am....for your loss. I know it's been a long time, but I still think about him. Often," he added.

Juanita stopped on the other side of the fence across from Mike and gave him an appraising look. Deciding he was not a danger to her, at least not in a physical sense, she reached out her hand. Whether he would be a danger to her in an emotional sense was yet to be determined. "Juanita Valdez," she said. "I'm pleased to meet you, even after all this time."

Mike extended his hand and shook Juanita's briefly. "Mike. Mike Spence," Mike said. "I didn't know if you and your husband still lived here or not. I was able to find your address in an old phone book. I don't mean to intrude."

"My husband died several years back. It's just me." She paused momentarily, a look of indecision on her face. Then, seeing the emotional anguish riding just beneath the surface of this stranger's face, she decided his emotional well-being was just as much at risk as hers. "Would you like to come up to the porch for a cup of coffee?" Juanita asked.

"Yes. Yes, I would," Mike replied.

Five minutes later they were settled in matching wooden chairs that resided on the small concrete porch to the right of the front door. Both held steaming cups of coffee, lost in silence that neither quite knew how to broach.

"Do you still work on the ambulance, Mr. Spence?" Juanita finally asked.

"Please, call me Mike," he replied. "No, I haven't done that in about twenty years. I'm in insurance now, mainly servicing of existing accounts. Office work mainly; pretty boring stuff."

"I see," Juanita replied. "I don't really remember you, from that day," she said hesitantly.

Mike draws in a deep breath. "When we arrived, the police were with you. We never spoke to you or your husband, I'm sorry to say. I remember seeing you, but I couldn't think of a way to offer you any comfort; no comfort can really help in these sorts of things, can they?"

"No," she replied, "it can't. Not in the moment."

Another moment of silence between them. Then, Juanita slowly said, "Joey was such a good boy. He loved school, was always curious about everything. He would ride his bike around the neighborhood, always exploring. That day... That day his dad was going to teach him to fish. We were planning a family vacation up at Lake Conroe, and Juan, my husband, wanted to show Joey, wanted to let him practice throwing in the line so he would be comfortable with it before the trip. So we went down to the river to practice fishing."

A tear slowly made a path down her face. "He wasn't supposed to get in the water. I specifically told him to stay at the edge. I stood back from the river, about twenty feet maybe, and watched both of them; Joey standing there with the rod, the fishing line in the water, pulling with the current, his father standing next to him. It was getting warm out and the mosquitoes were starting to bite. Juan slapped one of his arms, turned and said something to Joey, and then walked over to me. 'Got any bug spray in the truck?' he asked. I nodded, and we both walked the distance to the truck, about eighty feet from the edge of the water. We had pulled it up onto the dirt under the overpass.

"We were only gone for a couple of minutes. Our backs were turned only a few seconds to get the bug spray and some drinks out of the bed of the pickup, but when we turned back, Joey was gone.

"Panicked, we ran back to the edge of the water. He was nowhere to be seen. Juan waded into the river, but there was a sudden drop off only a couple of feet out, and he almost went completely under. He managed to get back to the shore before the current pulled him away.

"We think Joey must have slipped on the muddy edge, or maybe he took a step closer to try to see through the muddy water, and the current pulled him under and into the drop off."

She looked across at him, tears in both eyes. "It was only a couple of seconds," she repeated shakily.

"I'm sorry," Mike replied, the phrase feeling completely inadequate. "I wish there had been more we could have done to find your son. Believe me, Frank and I wanted to, but ambulances are not equipped for water rescues; that falls under the fire department, and they *were* doing everything they could to find him. If only they could have found him sooner."

"It's not your fault, Mike. I know everyone tried to help," Juanita answered.

There they were. Those words of absolution, the forgiveness he had craved all these years without realizing it. Some of the burden Mike had been carrying suddenly lifted and he was filled with relief. He still felt guilt from not being able to save Joey from that tragedy, however, this forgiveness from Jaunita eased it somewhat. Mike wondered, he hoped, that it also brought Juanita some peace.

"Thank you, Juanita. I hope after all this time you know it was not your fault either. It happened so fast that even if you had been standing nearby there would have been nothing you could have done. It's a miracle that your husband didn't get pulled under as well."

"I know," Juanita replied. "It's kind of you to say that."

"What happened to your husband?" Mike asked.

Juanita shook her head, a look of pain on her face. "He never got over the death of Joey; neither of us did. Juan felt completely responsible," she sighed. "I blamed him as well, and he knew it. At least at first, although with time comes acceptance, and forgiveness. But Juan couldn't forgive himself. He committed suicide about ten years ago."

Mike sat back. "Jeez, I'm so sorry, Juanita."

"It's ok. Thank you," she replied. Looking around, she continued, "I've stayed here all this time. It's not much, but it was our home together. I remember Joey playing in that yard, riding his bike up and down that sidewalk. I remember Juan working on that truck," she said, nodding towards the disabled pickup. "All I have left are my memories, and the good ones are still here." She hesitated, then – "if only we had made different choices that day."

Mike remained a while longer, both he and Juanita sipping on their coffees. Most of the time they were silent, reflective. Juanita asked Mike about his family, his job, and the weather. She had shared some of her painful memories with Mike, along with some of the good ones about her son, and in doing so, it seemed to help him in some way, and in return, that gave Juanita a small amount of comfort back.

He asked her if he could stop by again someday and she said that would be nice.

As Mike got in his car to leave with a smile and a wave to Juanita, he began to think. *What if we* had *made different choices that day?* Flexing his scarred hand against the steering wheel as he pulled away from the curb, he thought, *What if we* could *make different choices that day?*

Chapter Six

"How was your day, dear?" Sally asked. Mike had just returned home from his visit with Juanita.

"Pretty good. The usual I guess," Mike replied absently, heading into the bedroom.

After a quick check of the pizza in the oven, Sally headed after him. "Everything ok at the office?"

"I guess," Mike replied. He was at the sink, washing his hands, and glanced at her in the mirror.

"Mike. Your boss called me. He said you left early for an appointment. What appointment was that? What's going on?" she asked.

Mike turned toward her, smiling. "No appointment, actually. I just needed an extra hour off work, that's all. The workload has been light this month. It's not like I ditched the entire day."

"Why didn't you tell me?" she asked, not accusingly, just trying to understand.

"I didn't want to worry you, and I can tell by that look on your face now, you are worried," Mike said with a slight chuckle.

"Not funny, Mike. You know I worry. I want to help, but you need to let me inside once in a while to do so."

Mike walked over and gave her a hug. "I know, darling. I love you, more than you know." Stepping back he continued, "I've been thinking about Joey Valdez a lot lately; that's the kid that drowned in the Brazos."

"I didn't know you knew his name," Sally said.

"I didn't until the other day. I got Chuck Stevens to do me a solid and help me find the information. I wanted to pay my respects to his final resting spot, but just as important, I wanted to meet his folks, see how they are doing after all these years."

"Did you?" Sally asked.

"Well, I met his mom. His dad died years ago, suicide. The mom, Juanita, is managing. I can tell she never really got over it. I mean, can you imagine if our kid had..." he stopped, unable to continue.

"No. No I can't. But you know the doc says you can't fixate on things like that. Those 'what ifs' will just drive you crazy."

"I know, I know. I'm not. Honestly," he said sincerely. "It's just that, something happened in one of my blinks last week. The one about Joey's drowning. This scar," he said, holding up his hand, "I meant it when I said I couldn't remember how I got this." He hesitated, and then plunged in: "I think I got it *during* the blink. Somehow, I don't know, I did something I did not do all those years ago and it somehow changed things."

"Honey," Sally said quietly, "you have had that scar for a long time. I would know. I've seen every inch of your body."

"Yes, you would think that, because if I had somehow changed what happened, it would become part of my history, wouldn't it?" he asked.

Sally wasn't sure what to make of this conversation. It bordered on delusion. How could one change something in a flashback episode? The answer is: they can't. It's impossible. This had to be some form of the PTSD. It was different from what Mike usually experienced, but that had to be it.

"Listen, Mike. I think you need to get in to see the doc. You've been having more blinks recently, skipping out of work, looking up these people, and now this? I'm worried about you, hun, and with good reason. I think your PTSD is getting worse."

"You think I'm crazy, don't you?" Mike replied, suddenly feeling angry.

"No. Not at all. I just think you need some help. Go talk to the doc, ok?"

"Look, whatever is happening to me, it's not crazy. Ok, maybe it sounds crazy, but *I'm* not, ok? Just give me some time to work it out.

I'll be fine."

Sally sighed. "Reese is coming to visit this weekend. Try to work it out before then if you can. You know it bothers him when you get like this."

"I'm fine. Again, just give me some time."

• • • •

Later that night, Sally was asleep and Mike was downstairs on the sofa, thinking.

Ok, so let's cover what I know, he mused. *The kid, Joey, goes practice-fishing with his parents at the river turnaround. Somehow, he falls or gets in the water and drowns. Frank and I make the call but there is nothing we can do. That's what happened.*

I've blinked about this call off and on for years, and thought about it even more. Recently, I blinked into the Brazos call and hit a pile of junk with my fist, causing a laceration to the back of my hand.' Reaching down, he rubs the scar. *'The one that caused this scar.*

That was new. That did not happen on the original call; the "origin call" let's say. It only happened during the blink, but somehow, I don't know how, it became real.

So, what if? What if I can force myself back to that moment? I was thinking about it in the office when I blinked back, and that was different; the flashbacks have always been random without a trigger, but what if I triggered it this time? What if I can try to change something else? Will that also become real? Can I somehow stop the kid, Joey, from entering the water? If I do that then he never drowns. I never hit the junk that caused this scar. And Joey's dad doesn't commit suicide. Is that even possible?

Mike continued to rub absently at his hand scar. *I've never tried to force a blink before.*

Mike leaned back against the sofa. *The only way to know is to try,* he decided. He closed his eyes, scooting his butt down on the cushion to get in a more comfortable position.

It was quiet in the house. Sal was asleep upstairs. He could hear the faint ticking of the clock on the wall. All else was still, silent. He slowed his breathing, deeply, in and out. He began to think back to that day, not to the incident, but to earlier. Back to when they were still at the station. It was around mid-day. Frank was in the kitchen making a sandwich and Mike was flipping channels on the television...

"Find a movie," Frank calls from the kitchen. "There's usually good action flicks on Sunday afternoons." No immediate answer from Mike. "Mike, you hear?"

Mike has paused in his searching. Something feels off but for a moment he is not quite sure what it is. Maybe it's hearing Frank's voice again, so clear, so... real. Like he is right there in the other room. But Mike knows Frank is dead and buried, and has been for years.

"Yeah, I hear ya," Mike replies.

He did it, he thinks. He forced a flashback, a blink. Not only that, he is *aware that he's in a blink. That's never happened before either.* This may actually work. *Looking down at his right hand, he sees clear skin, no scar.* It hasn't happened yet, *he thinks excitedly.*

"Frank, we need to go," Mike says, standing up and tossing the remote control on the couch.

Frank walks into the living area, a plate in hand, chips piled high next to his bologna and cheese sandwich. "Go where? I just made lunch, man," he answers.

"I can't explain, but we need to take a drive. It won't take long. Come on, let's go," Mike says. He is already heading for the door to the bay, where the truck is parked nose out, waiting for the next emergency.

"Seriously?" Frank asks. He can see that Mike is dead serious. He's heading to the bay with a purpose; he's got his medic-face on, as Frank likes to call it. That look when you are on a call, full focus, full attention on what is going on around you. Mike is in the "zone."

He quickly back-steps into the kitchen, sets his plate in the fridge, and heads to the garage bay. Mike has already pulled out the truck and is sitting with the engine idling, still in gear. As soon as Frank clears the garage bay door he hears it begin to close behind him. "Damn he's in a hurry," he says to himself.

Frank climbs into the passenger seat, and Mike starts rolling as soon as his feet are off the ground. "Whoa, man, let me get in first, ok? Shit, what's the rush?"

"I can't explain," Mike says. He thinks quickly, I can't tell him what is really happening, he will think I'm nuts. But I need to offer him something.

"Look, it's just a hunch, but we need to get down to the river turnaround. I think something bad is about to happen. I heard the recent rains have made the river run harder than normal, and I just want to check down there, ok?"

Frank shrugs. "All right. An ounce of prevention and all that. I'll let dispatch know we are out on rounds," he says, picking up the mic. It's not unusual for an ambulance crew to patrol their district, or make rounds, as it helps them memorize the roadways and, with the expansion the county is seeing, there are always new roads and subdivisions to learn.

Mike slows briefly at the driveway before turning onto Williams Trace Boulevard, where the station is located. They are only a block from the highway that leads to the river, but Mike can see there are at least a couple traffic signal cycles before they will clear the intersection. He doesn't think they have that much time.

Remembering back, it occurs to him that Frank was just about finished with his lunch when they got the call for the possible drowning. When they had previously arrived on scene, it was about twenty minutes after the kid went in the water. That means it could be happening right now.

Mike reaches over and flips the switches to activate the emergency lights, then hits the siren switch. The fast sounding wee-wah wee-wah begins.

"Dude, what are you doing?" Franks asks.

"There is no time," Mike replies. "Just let me drive."

Mike deftly steers the unit to the left into the oncoming traffic lanes, as all the lanes facing the intersection are full of vehicles. He does this carefully but with purpose, giving only the briefest pause for the oncoming traffic to slow and pull over out of the way.

Reaching the intersection, and with a quick look in all directions to make sure other drivers have seen them and stopped, Mike veers in front of the traffic and heads under the overpass. A brief stop on the other side and then he's turning left, accelerating onto the access road and heading for the on ramp, about half a mile ahead.

Something is off about this, *Frank thinks, but keeps his opinion to himself. He's worked with Mike for a few years now. Although Mike hasn't been in EMS as long as Frank has, he trusts him, trusts his judgment. They can read each other on calls and know what the other medic needs before they ask for it most of the time. He decides he just has to trust Mike now, even though his behavior seems a bit, well,* erratic *would be a good word for it.*

They have entered the freeway now, and Mike has really punched it, getting the truck up to a solid eighty miles per hour. They are in the left lane, and traffic is pulling left and right to give them passage.

We are out of time, *Mike thinks to himself.* Have to get there in time. *Stomping on the accelerator, he pushes the truck to ninety.*

"A little fast, bro," Frank states calmly. He's used to driving fast, but this is at the red line.

"We'll be fine," Mike replies curtly.

Up ahead is the off ramp to the turnaround. The sign, Brazos River Turnaround, white reflective letters on standard green background, flashes by in a blur. There is an eighteen-wheeler up ahead on the right, not slowing down or pulling over. Probably has his radio blaring and doesn't hear the fucking siren. If Mike slows and gets behind him, he will lose precious seconds. I can get past him, *Mike determines.*

Accelerating even more, Mike pulls up alongside the truck. Now the driver hears him and begins applying the airbrakes, and the truck quickly begins to drop back. The exit ramp is just ahead, maybe a hundred yards, no distance at all at these speeds.

Mike glances in the right side mirror, and as soon as the large truck has cleared the rear of the ambulance, he pulls the steering wheel to the right, cutting in front of the big truck with only feet to spare, and takes the exit ramp.

"Jesus, man! What the fuck?" Frank yells. He's pissed now. It's one thing to do a wellness check somewhere, it's entirely another to drive like a bat out of hell to get there.

Mike ignores the outburst from his partner. He's on the access road headed to the turnaround now and the road is completely clear. Not too many drivers come down here as it only makes a U-turn to get back on the freeway heading the other direction.

Mike kills the siren but leaves the lights on. Up ahead is a left-hand turn that will take them under the bridge. A traffic barricade, red and white angled stripes, is in front of them, indicating the roadway does not continue straight.

He brakes, slowing the truck down to thirty, and makes the turn. Up ahead is an empty roadway, about three hundred feet long, that then makes another sharp left on the opposite side of the underpass. No vehicles are on the road ahead but Mike spots a pickup truck off the road, about two hundred feet from the curb. It looks to be the same truck he saw at Juanita's the other day, but with all four wheels intact.

Further to his right, he sees a man and woman walking towards the vehicle. Turning his head slightly more, he sees a small figure standing at the edge of the river bank.

Slamming on the brakes and ramming the ambulance in park, he leaps out of the driver's seat, not bothering to shut down the engine. In time, but barely, *Mike thinks.* It will happen quickly, and once he goes in he will be gone.

Mike bolts towards the kid, which will also take him right past the parents. He's running as fast as he can and the adrenaline has kicked in to help.

"Hey!" he yells out. "Get away from there!"

The man and woman stop, staring. They don't know who this guy is yelling at. All they see is this man in a blue uniform running towards them. The uniform looks like a cop, complete with a badge, but the woman sees the ambulance, so she associates him with it as an ambulance driver.

Her husband, who doesn't care much for cops, having been in trouble more times than he cares to remember as a youth, is tunnel-visioned on the man. "What is this?" Juan Valdez exclaims. His hackles are up now, triggered by an emotional response from past experiences when guys just like this white guy, in similar uniforms, would chase him and his compadres. His mind closes out the fact that there is a white ambulance, blue stripes wrapped around the side, red and white lights flashing and strobing, and only sees the man, a threat, running towards him and his wife.

Juan steps in front of his wife and puts up both hands, balling them into fists, to protect against this threat.

Mike, running at breakneck speed, sees the man step towards him, in front of the woman. His fists are up. He sees this in an instant, just a fast glance in that direction, as all of his attention is on the boy, still standing on the bank, one hundred feet ahead of him. His work boots are not made for sprinting, and his running feels a bit clunky, but at least the ground is mostly dry. The expanse under the large freeway overpass shelters the barren dirt from most of the overhead rain but there are some damp puddles from the runoff spouts.

Mike swerves left to avoid the worst of these, which puts him on a direct path with the man and woman. He's still focused on the boy but turns to the parents.

"Get him away from there!" Mike cries out.

At this point, the lady – he sees it is a younger version of Juanita, the haggard widow he met recently – begins to turn away, shifting her head to *the left, to look back towards her son at the river's edge. The man, however, is still focused on Mike, who is running directly at him. He pulls back his hand to throw a punch, thinking he is being attacked.*

Mike clears the puddle and adjusts his course back to the right, directly towards the kid. It's just enough to prevent bowling over the man, but not enough to prevent the glancing blow from the fist. As he runs past, the man's right fist, aimed for his head, strikes his left shoulder, knocking Mike off balance.

Mike stumbles, falling forward, his head still up, his eyes still focused on the boy, who hasn't moved. Yet.

A searing pain in his right hand as Mike strikes the ground. He's not sure what he caught it on, but the fire he feels tells him it's bad. Mike puts that in the background as he rolls, carried forward by the momentum of his running, and is quickly back on his feet. Clear of the man, he has a direct run to the kid, now sixty feet in front of him.

He's winded now and can't catch enough breath to yell.

Thirty feet. The boy hasn't heard the commotion behind him, or has ignored it, fascinated with his first attempt at fishing. He's now glancing down, looking at the water. He thinks he sees something, maybe a turtle or a snake.

Twenty feet. The boy starts leaning forwards, fishing pole in his right hand, reaching with his left.

Ten feet away now. Mike starts to slow his approach, afraid he'll tackle the kid and they will both go in. Dampness running down his right hand; the fire still there, but forgotten for the moment.

The boy leans even further over the river's edge, reaching down, grabbing at something. Just then, his right foot slips on the soft mud at the edge of the bank, his foot shifting forward into the rapidly moving murky waters. He pinwheels with his arms, dropping the pole, as he feels the cold water on this right calf.

A vice grip grabs his left arm, pulling him backwards. He doesn't know what has him, but it is causing pain. Suddenly he's on his back, looking up at the underside of the bridge overhead; the clunk clunk of vehicles going over the roadway seams sounding with an echoing quality, like a distant drum. To his left, also on the ground, is a man, panting, staring at him.

Sitting up, he looks around and sees his parents running towards him, another man coming up behind them.

Joey's attention is drawn back to the man next to him, who speaks in a rasping voice.

Mike stares at the boy. It's the same boy from his nightmares, his flashbacks, only this time he's not motionless on the ground with white foam and water pouring from his mouth. This time he is not the ashen gray of the dead. This time, he's alive, breathing, looking at him. "Are you ok?" Mike asks in a rasping voice, still trying to catch his breath.

The boy nods silently, shifting himself slightly away from this stranger.

"Joey!" Juanita cries, coming up to her son. "Are you ok, did this man hurt you?" she asks.

By now, Juan is standing over Mike, a look of anger in his eyes. "What are you doing, man?" he asks, his hands still balled into fists.

Frank is seconds behind him. "It's ok, it's ok," he says. "We're medics! Everyone calm down!"

Juan looks over at Frank, seeing him for the first time. The blue uniform with the badge, so like a cop, but he can now see the star of life emblem on the badge, and on the shoulder patch, silver and blue, with the words Emergency Medical Services around the edge. He loosens his hands, looks back down at the man on the ground. His shirt is dirty from the fall, and his right hand is a bloody mess, but he can see now that the man is a medic.

Slowly, Juan reaches down with his right hand open, offering to help Mike up.

Mike grasps the offered hand with his left, non-bloodied hand, and slowly gets to his feet, looking between the man and woman and their son, Joey, who is still alive.

"Thanks," Mike says. "Sorry if I scared you. I spotted your son by the edge there, and was afraid he was going to fall in. The recent rains north of here have made the river swell and there are dangerous undercurrents."

"He grabbed me, Mom. I slipped," Joey says, standing and moving over to his mom. "See, my leg is all wet!"

Juanita looks from her son to Mike, realization spreading across her face. She understands how close she just came to possibly losing her son. "Thank you. Thank you for being here. But how did you know?"

Mike hesitates and looks over to Frank, who is looking at him with the same question written on his face. "I didn't, really," Mike answers. "I just know the rains can make this spot dangerous so we came to check. A kid drowned here once a long time ago." A long time ago for me, *Mike thinks.*

"Well," Juanita says, "we are grateful for your help. We were just practicing fishing."

I know, *Mike almost says, but stops himself at the last moment. The fire in his hand is becoming more urgent, the wetness still there. Mike glances down and sees that he's ripped a large laceration into his hand. He must have caught it on debris when he fell.*

"Sorry about that, man," Juan is saying. "I didn't know who you were and you were just running towards us."

"It's ok; completely understandable," Mike assures him.

Frank steps up and takes a look at Mike's hand, lifting it up by the arm to keep away from the blood. "Nasty. Let's get back to the truck and get that cleaned up," he says.

Mike nods and then turns to Joey. The kid is looking up at him, smiling. It's the best smile he thinks he has ever seen. Mike sticks out his left hand, since the right one is bloody, and the kid shakes it. "I'm Mike."

"I'm Joey," the boy says.

The clock was still ticking away, the house was still quiet. The only thing that changed was the position of the clock's delicate hands; they had moved ever so slightly, perhaps a minute, perhaps two.

Mike opened his eyes. He stared straight ahead at the wall for a moment, not sure where he was or what he was doing. Then he remembered; he remembered it all. *I really may have done it.*

Looking down, he sees the ugly scar on the back of his hand, like a crooked evil clown smile. *Well, I ended up with this thing after all,* he thinks, an uncomfortable feeling in his chest.

• • • •

Morning. The smell of freshly cooked bacon wafted on the air as Sally came downstairs. She saw Mike in the kitchen, a yellow apron around his waist, scrambling some eggs.

"Morning," she said. "You're up early."

"Morning," Mike replied. "Coffee is ready. Want a cup?"

"Sure. Thanks," she said as he brought her a hot cup of black java. *He's excited about something. I see that look in his eye, the way he's grinning.* "What's going on, Mike?"

His smile widened. "I think something wonderful has happened; crazy, but wonderful."

Sally sat down at the breakfast table. "I'm all ears," she said.

Mike came into the breakfast nook, placing a plate full of scrambled eggs and bacon in front of her and another on his side of the small, round table. He went back for his coffee cup, then sat. He could hardly contain his excitement.

"I think I changed it, Sal," he said.

"What?" Sally said, around a mouthful of eggs.

"The drowning, the kid in the Brazos. I think I changed it," Mike said excitedly.

Sally paused, looking up at him. "Mike, what drowning?"

"*The* drowning, Sal. The one at the turnaround. The one that I have flashbacks about?" he said.

"Hun, I have no idea what you are talking about. I'm sorry, but you never talked about a drowning at that spot before. Are you sure you have the location right? Is this a new blink you have not experienced before?"

For a moment Mike was confused. He'd told the story about the kid to Sal many times, it was one of the more common blinks he had; how the feeling of helplessness had stuck with him, the guilt at not being able to do anything.

Wait a second, he thought. *This is just further proof that I changed it! Of course she won't remember it, it never happened! And if it never happened, I never told her about it!*

"Ok. That actually makes sense, you not knowing," he said. "Let me try to explain."

Sally listened intently as Mike told her about this boy, Joey, who drowned at the Brazos turnaround. He said it was a call he and Frank were on together; the fire department couldn't find the boy, and it turned into a body recovery. Sally, hearing this story for the first time, tried to keep the look of concern off of her face. Mike had always shared his blinks with her, why would he have not shared this one if it was so frequent, so traumatizing? She couldn't believe what he said next.

"Somehow, I've found a way to alter what happens during the flashback. See, it started with this scar on my hand, it used to not be there, and then suddenly it was." He was talking faster now, trying to get it all out before she interrupted him. He could see the look of concern and disbelief on her face, although she was trying to remain neutral. "So, I thought, what if I could get there a few minutes sooner, and prevent Joey from going in the water? If I could do that, he would never drown. He would still be alive out there today! Isn't that incredible?"

"Honey," Sally began, setting her cup down.

"Wait, wait!" Mike said, raising his voice. "Let me finish. That's what I did last night! I was able to force the blink to happen, back to that moment in time, and I stopped the kid from going in the water. I saved him, don't you see?" Mike was anxious, fearful she wouldn't believe him. Why would she? It did sound pretty crazy, even to him.

"You don't believe me, do you?" he asked.

Sally took a moment before responding. "Honey, you believe it and that's what is important. I can see this is troubling you, but you've never shared this story about some kid drowning in the Brazos." She paused, "I think we need to call Doctor Birachi, hun. You have been having more blinks than normal. You seem anxious and I know you are not sleeping well. Reese is coming in tonight; you could talk to him, that always seems to help."

Mike took a deep breath. He couldn't explain this to Dr. Birachi; the doc really would think he was losing it. Worst case scenario was that he would prescribe some of those medications again; they always make him feel fuzzy, and it was difficult to concentrate while on them. While they had helped to control the flashbacks in the past, what if this time Mike *needed* the flashbacks? What if he could change things for more people?

"Look, I'll talk with our son. You're right, he has a way of helping to calm me down, as do you. But no doc yet, ok? This is important. I know it's hard to believe, but I really think I'm onto something wonderful here."

She smiled resignedly at him. "Ok, hun. I know you have ways of managing this. I'm just worried about you."

"How about when Reese is here we all take a drive? I think I can prove what is happening."

Sally sighed and nodded. "Sure. Let's do that."

· · · ·

Reese arrived at the house around dinner time. They ate a meal of pizza and salad, one of Reese's favorites, and heard about the current semester at school. Reese was in good spirits, having received an A on a recent paper and having recently met a young lady that he had taken an interest in.

"Just don't let her distract you too much from your studies," his father said with a quick wink and a smile.

"I won't, Dad," Reese replied, with his own wink and grin.

After dinner, they retired to the living room where Mike explained the recent flashbacks, and how he had prevented Joey's tragic mishap.

"Dad, that's incredible," Reese said. "But like Mom, I've never heard about this drowning before." He paused for a moment, with a thoughtful look on his face. "However, it does make sense that neither of us would remember it. Essentially, you are saying you changed the timeline, and since the incident never happened, you never would have spoken about it, would you? I mean, it is strange that you can still remember it and we can't but maybe that's because you were there at the pivotal moment that it changed. Essentially, you have experienced both timelines personally, whereas we only experienced it through your memory of the event. As it never happened in *this* timeline, you never shared the memory of it with us. This is all very Sci-Fi channel stuff, Dad," he finished with a smile.

"I know, right?" Mike said. "So do you believe me or am I going crazy?"

"Well, Dad, you've always been a little off," Reese said with another wink. "I just don't see how you can convince anyone else that something happened over two decades ago when there won't be any evidence of it. All the evidence will point to the current timeline of events."

"But I'll know the differences, even if no one else will. That's enough to really drive someone nuts," Mike said quietly. "Let's leave it there until tomorrow. Maybe I can show you something that will convince you."

• • • •

Saturday morning. After a hearty breakfast of pancakes and sausage, Mike, Sally, and Reese took a drive, Mike behind the wheel.

They stopped across the street from a house in Stafford. To Reese and Sally, it looked ordinary, like all the other houses on the block. Older home, well kept, looked like a recent coat of paint on the exterior, a pleasant beige. The yard was well kept, a flower garden in front of the entry. There was a Ford F-150 in the driveway, Valdez Paint and Home Repair proudly displayed on the driver's door. A small sedan was parked in front of the truck.

"I was here the other day, guys," Mike said softly. "That house," he pointed across the street, "was a rundown mess. It looked like it was dying a slow death, as did the lady that lived there. She was a widow, her husband having passed away several years ago, and her son, Joey, had drowned at the Brazos river turnaround twenty-two years ago. I talked to her briefly; nice lady, but haggard, just kind of existing. She didn't remember me from that day as I really didn't have any contact with her or her husband.

"But in the blink I triggered, I *did* have contact with them. In fact, I almost ran them over trying to get to Joey in time. I know it's been decades, but I wonder if she will remember me now?" Mike asked of no one in particular.

"Honey, you can't just show up out of the blue like this," Sally said, somewhat uneasily. "What if they don't remember you, or worse, what if you find that this never really happened? Are you sure you want to know?"

"I think I *have* to know, Sal. Am I going crazy, or did I somehow affect a change in the past?"

"Ok, just don't expect too much," she said.

Reese wasn't sure what to think. His dad said he was here just a few days ago at a ramshackle house, but he was sitting across from a very well-kept home; can that really have changed? Or was his father living in some sort of delusional hallucination? Were they enabling him by going along with this, or should they push back on his lack of willingness to go see his doctor? It could be a delicate balance with someone with PTSD; you needed to be understanding but also ensure they remain safe.

"I'll come with you, Dad," Reese said. "But first, I need you to promise us something. No matter what happens, whether they remember you or not, I think Mom is right and you need to see the doc this week. Just go talk through some of this with him, it might help. Ok?"

Mike looked between his son and wife. "I know you want to believe me. I also know why it's difficult. So, ok, I'll go," Mike said. "Now, let's go meet the Valdez family."

Mike and Reese walked across the street to the chain link fence surrounding the house. Sally waited in the car, not fully convinced in the endeavor but willing to see how it played out. Suddenly, she thought that it might be better if she were with them. It might look less intimidating to see a woman in the group of strangers walking up to your front door. Opening the car, she quickly joined her husband and son.

Mike gave the door a soft knock and took a step back, so that someone looking out the side window had a clear view of him. It always made him a little nervous standing at a door after what happened to Frank, and he was a bit surprised he was doing it, especially with his family. But it was daylight and none of them were going to do anything threatening, so there was no reason to feel anxious. Of course, Mike did anyway.

Right about the time Sally joined them, standing slightly to the side of her husband, the drapes on the window to the right of the door pulled back briefly and then fell into place. A woman about Sally's age opened the door halfway. "Yes?" she asked.

"Hi, um..." Mike began. He could see that the lady was Juanita Valdez, the same lady he met the other day, but she looked completely different. Her hair was pulled back into a ponytail, and she was wearing jeans and a nice blouse; colorful, with flowers on it.

"I'm sorry to bother you so early on a Saturday, but my name is

Mike Spence; I was a medic with the county years ago, and we met once. It was when you and your family were down at the Brazos and Joey almost fell in the water..." Mike trailed off, not sure what else to say. Suddenly, though, his anxiety turned to relief as he saw recognition in her eyes.

"Oh yes, you do look familiar. You...you are the one that came charging at us like a mad bull, aren't you?"

Mike let out a large breath of air he hadn't known he was holding. "Yea, that was me." He grinned.

"What can I do for you, mister..." Juanita started.

"Mike, Mike Spence," he said, reaching out his hand. "And this is my family, my wife Sally, and son, Reese. I know this is going to sound crazy but, we were in the area, and I was thinking about that time and telling my family about it, and well, I just thought I'd stop by and see how you and Joey are doing. I remembered your name and looked up your address so, well, here we are," Mike finished.

Juanita reached out and briefly shook everyone's hand. "Pleased to meet you. We are all good, Mr. Spence. Joey's not here, he's in the military and currently overseas, but he is doing well; just made Captain. My husband is in the shower, getting ready for work. He owns his own business," she said, nodding towards the truck, "and has a big project he is finishing up, otherwise I would invite you in."

"No, no, that's quite alright," Mike replied. "I'm just thrilled that you remembered, and to finally meet you under better circumstances."

They exchanged a few more pleasantries before heading back to the car.

Reese turned to his dad. "Dad, I'm glad she remembered you. That proves part of your story that there was almost an incident and it obviously was impactful enough that she remembered you, even after all this time." He paused. "But, it doesn't prove the other part; that Joey drowned and you went back in time and stopped it. Like I said last night, if you changed the timeline, that means it didn't happen in the first place. Don't forget, you promised to see the doc this week," he reminded his father.

Mike was elated that at least part of his story had been proven to his family. He hadn't made the entire thing up. And he knew in his heart that he changed the course of this family's life, everything from the kid surviving to his father still being around and running a business. Even Juanita seemed better – happy and, well, just normal. Like she hadn't suffered the pain and loss of losing her son and husband, because in fact, Mike had prevented those things from happening.

He started to wonder, *Could I do it again?*

"I know, son. I did promise and I'll call him first thing Monday for an appointment. Thank you both for trying to believe."

· · · ·

Doctor Birachi's office was located in an upscale section of Houston, near the famous Galleria shopping center. It was on the tenth floor of an office building, with a nice view of a city park below.

Birachi was able to get him in mid-week for a session. A combat veteran, Birachi served during Desert Storm as an infantryman, and after his tour of duty and obligation to Uncle Sam had ended he felt a calling to become a psychologist specializing in PTSD cases, mainly veterans who had trouble adjusting back to civilian life after the war. He also had quite a following of public service employees, ranging from police officers to fire and health care workers.

His office had an adjoining conversation area that looked more like a living room than a doctor's office. It was designed to instill a sense of calm and familiarity to his patients. He found that keeping people relaxed, in a non-formal setting, was the first step in getting them to open up and talk. And by talking, he could best assess what treatment options would potentially help the most.

"Mike," Birachi said, "good to see you. It's been a while, hasn't it?"

"Morning, Doc. Thanks for seeing me on short notice. Sorry I've stayed away so long."

"Well, usually that's a good sign, my patients staying away. That means I've helped," Birachi answered. "Let's have a seat in here," he said, motioning to the adjoining room.

Mike sat himself on the leather recliner, while Dr. Birachi took the sofa.

"Doc, what do you know about altering time and space?" Mike began.

Half an hour later Mike had finished telling Birachi what he had been experiencing. He ended with retelling of his meeting with Juanita, as a reaffirmation that his tinkering with the past through his flashback resulted in a great outcome for the entire Valdez family.

Birachi kept quiet while Mike spoke, nodding and prompting him to continue when Mike would stop. He had his laptop open on a small stand in front of him, and would occasionally lean forward and type in a few notes.

"That's quite a tale, Mike," Birachi commented when Mike finally leaned back in his chair, finished. "How are you feeling right now?" he asked.

"I feel really great," Mike replied. "I mean, something good has finally come of all these flashbacks and bad memories. My family thinks I may be going nuts, but honestly, I feel really good. What do you think?"

"Well, Mike, the flashbacks are your body's way of dealing with the repressed stress of those traumatic times you experienced in the past. It is your body coping. If you accept them for what they are, it will help you get past them. On the surface, as a medical provider, I must say I'm thinking that your recent manifestations of the flashbacks, and your desire to modify the outcome, is your emotional state trying to further suppress the stress, instead of trying to heal from it.

"It is very likely the anniversary of Frank's death has triggered the increase in episodes, and this is your way of dealing with the increase. Once that tragic anniversary has passed, you may find the PTSD returns to more normal levels, and your subconsciousness will no longer feel the need to suppress these emotions and feelings."

"So you think my efforts to suppress the stress, the flashbacks, are trying to suppress themselves even further? A suppression of the suppression, in other words?" Mike asked.

"Essentially, that is correct." Birachi hesitated. "Now, let's dig a little deeper. Let's assume that what you are feeling is actually happening. That you somehow have gone into your memories and triggered a change. I think you need to consider the possible outcomes to such an endeavor."

"What do you mean?"

"Have you ever heard of the butterfly effect?" Birachi asked. "It's a phenomenon that a mathematician in the early '60s discovered when running computer models to predict the path of tornados. He discovered that the slightest change in the math predicting the weather patterns could have a dramatic change in the outcome, and essentially compared it to a butterfly flapping its wings having the ability to dramatically alter the outcome of something as powerful as a tornado.

"By the same token, assuming you changed something in the past, however small, you could be dramatically impacting future events in ways that may not even have occurred yet. In this case, you saved the boy, leading to the boy and his father still being alive today, and apparently leading successful lives. But, what if, let's say, one of them being alive today somehow led to the death of someone else, or on a larger scale, a world war? What if this Joey kid, now in the military, is going to decide to wipe out a village in some foreign country, or he pushes the button that starts a nuclear war? It may seem far-fetched, but it should be considered as part of your decision to alter the past.

"Beyond that, however, consider fate. What if Joey was destined to die that day? What if, by altering that fact, you are simply delaying the inevitable? Those who believe in fate believe that the universe will eventually correct itself of any alterations in destiny, so maybe you saved him for a few years, but maybe his eventual fate will be worse than the original one. Maybe he will be captured overseas by the enemy to be tortured and eventually killed. Isn't that worse than what happened to him originally?

"Finally, I would ask you to consider God. For those with strong religious beliefs, there is generally an idea that the next life will be better than this one. That when what we perceive as a tragedy strikes, it is simply God's will to bring one of his children home to Him. If you are altering the past and preventing God's calling, are you altering the will of God, or somehow denying Him something which is rightfully His?"

Birachi took a moment to let all this sink in. "I'm not saying any of these ideas are right or wrong, I am merely posing alternatives and theories. It's up to you to decide which may be applicable, or if none are. I'm saying if you believe you have actually altered the past, you must also consider the consequences of such actions, acknowledge that while this outcome appears positive, they may not all be that way, and you will live with the consequences of those actions as surely as you live with the consequences of your past."

Mike let it all absorb for a moment. He wasn't a huge believer in God, or fate, or karma, or destiny. He had always been a realist. He believed in the here and now, what he could see, feel, and touch. He believed in helping people; after all, that was why he became a medic in the first place, to help people. If there was a God with divine powers, He would have more peaceful ways of calling His flock home other than shootings, stabbings, drownings, and car wrecks.

What the doc had said about the butterfly effect, however, having a ripple effect from one moment to a future one – that may have some merit. After all, think about all the people that Joey has encountered since his near miss with death, the opportunities for positive influence that he has had. Just the positive outcome his being here, alive, has had on his family makes it right. That made it all worthwhile, even if something such as fate should intervene later, doesn't it?

"That makes sense, doc," Mike said. "I'll give that some consideration, although I don't know if it will prevent me from trying again. If you think about it, by talking with you, should I decide to suppress this and just go with the next flashback and not try to modify it, you have essentially altered *my* course and destiny the same as that butterfly."

Birachi nodded and smiled. "Good point, Mike."

The rest of the visit went quickly. Birachi asked Mike if he was having trouble sleeping or concentrating, how his relationship was with Sally and Reese, did he need anything to help him sleep or cope with stress, the usual doctor questions. Mike politely answered in the usual back and forth doctor-patient conversation; sleeping well (small lie), concentrating well (actually a bit distracted but he didn't need to know that), things were good at home, no meds needed, etc.

Mike ended up promising Birachi that he would reach out to him, day or night, if he needed anything, even just to talk. It was reassuring to know he had this guy as part of his support network, but at the end of the day, Mike believed he was doing something good, and planned to try again, tonight. He knew just the call to try it on.

Chapter Seven

Mike opened his eyes and looked over at the clock: 2 a.m. Rolling his head to the left, he saw Sal's deep breaths indicating that she was sound asleep. He had lain in bed for two hours waiting for the sound of deep, regular breathing just to ensure she was in deep sleep.

Time to move. He got up slowly, walked into the living room, and gently sat in his favorite armchair. He kept the lights off.

Slowing his own breathing, he began to think back. He recalled the accidental shooting, the cramped space they had to work on him, and how ultimately, it had been determined that John Cray was brain-dead. Mike remembered reading an article in the newspaper about a week after Cray's death promoting organ donation registration, as his harvested organs had gone to help four other people who benefited from his eyes, liver, and kidneys.

Mike had been contemplating those four organ recipients, and wondering if he was about to make a butterfly flap its wings and cause a tornado-like impact in those four lives. *Surely those people will get organs from another person, right?* he mused. *Saving Cray is not a death sentence for any of them. Doesn't John Cray deserve a chance to live and be with his family if I can give him that?*

Mike thought back to earlier that day. He and Frank had been returning from a call...

They're on Highway Six, a six-lane roadway that runs north and south between Highway Ninety in Sugar Land and northwest Houston. It has become a major thoroughfare in the past ten years, with residential communities both east and west of it. The roadway itself is littered with strip centers and fast food eateries. The increased development has brought increased traffic, and with the traffic, increased accidents.

The one they just left was a minor accident with no injuries. The traffic light on Six had turned green, the lead vehicle started to move, and then stopped hard when another driver made a fast dash across the intersection, thinking to make the yellow light but instead crossing on red. The sudden stop resulted in the trailing vehicle bumping into the first one. There was only minor damage to both vehicles. Both drivers said they were fine, so Frank quickly got the ambulance back in service and they headed back towards the station.

Mike is driving, as it is Frank's turn to run the call.

"Hey, Frank, going to make a quick stop if that's ok with you," Mike says. He knows the Cray family lives off of Six, just up ahead in the Pheasant Creek neighborhood.

"Sure. Where to?" Frank asks.

Time to let him in on my little secret? *Mike asks himself.* I'm not sure how to explain this otherwise. Or should I just make some shit up?

Mike goes for making some shit up. "There's this guy lives near here. I don't know him very well, but I heard he recently purchased a firearm for home protection. I'm in the market as well so I thought I'd run by and check it out."

"You wanna get a gun?" Franks asks, surprised.

"Yeah, you know, for protection."

Mike makes the turn into the neighborhood, trying to remember the exact route. Let's see, it was a right, left, then right to a cul-de-sac, *he thinks. Making the navigation, he sees Sugar Way Court up on the right.* Yep, that's it.

Turning, he slowly drives down the short street to the cul-de-sac, looking at houses on both sides.

"You sure you know where this guy lives?" Frank asks, watching as Mike looks from left to right.

"Yep. It's that one," Mike says, nodding to the red brick house on the right. He pulls up and puts the unit in park. "Hey, would you mind waiting here? I won't be long."

"No problem, man."

Mike steps out of the vehicle, leaving the engine idling so Frank has some air conditioning and can listen to music on the radio. He heads up the walk to the front door.

Need to play this cool, *Mike thinks.* Just go with the plan that I thought of while waiting for Sal to nod off.

Mike rings the doorbell and a moment later a big guy cracks the door open a few inches. He sees Mike standing there in uniform, looks past him to see the ambulance sitting at his curb. Looking back to Mike, he determines there is no threat (one can never be too careful with all the recent home invasions), and opens the door all the way.

"Can I help you?" John Cray asks.

"Yes. My name is Mike Spence and I work with the county ambulance service. You may not know this, but whenever a resident purchases a firearm, we get notified and are asked to stop by and do a safety check. Do you mind if I come in, Mr. Cray?" Mike reasons he knows enough information to trick John into thinking this is official county business and that would get him access to the home and the gun. Then he would caution John on how to safely store it.

John looks at him sideways, narrowing his eyes. "Never heard of that before. But this is my first purchase so I guess I wouldn't have, huh?"

John steps to the side of the door. "Come on in," he says. John extends his hand and shakes Mike's as he enters, then closes the door behind him.

"Bought it for home security. Lots of nasty things happening in the city recently, you know?" John takes Mike through the living room, kitchen, and into a small laundry area. Mike recognizes the laundry area, although he is approaching it from the interior, not the garage like he will later tonight.

"Can't be too careful, I know," Mike says. "We want to make sure things are buttoned up though so that we don't have to pay an unnecessary visit. Lot of accidents happen with firearms, especially with new owners. Although I'm sure you are very careful."

"I sure am," John replies. "Since I just got it, I haven't had a chance to get a storage locker yet, so I'm keeping it in here up high, away from my kids. I got all the safety bases covered that way."

So you think, *Mike says to himself. You don't know what's coming later tonight.*

John stops and begins to reach up for the Remington.

"Hold up," Mike says suddenly. "Do you mind if I get it? I'm a bit particular about doing these sorts of things."

"Be my guest," John says. "But be careful, it's loaded."

Mike steps past John and looks up at the overhead shelf. He can just see the barrel sticking past the edge of the shelf. It's a bit high for Mike, and he doesn't want to reach up blindly. "Listen, do you have a step ladder I could use?"

"Sure, it's in the garage. Let me get it." Cray opens the door behind him leading to the garage, steps out briefly, and returns with a two-step ladder, setting it up for Mike.

"Thanks," Mike says.

Mike steps up on the ladder so he can be eye level with the shelf. Now he can see the gleaming black barrel of the shotgun, and using both hands, reaches out and gently picks it up, pulls it to his chest, and steps back to ground level.

"Remington pump action. Nice one," Mike says. "I love the scrollwork on the barrel, and the wooden stock is a nice deep brown color. You said it's loaded. Is there a round in the chamber?"

"Damn straight there is. I want to be able to grab and shoot, you know?"

"I can understand that. Looks like the safety is off as well. Listen, did they mention when you purchased this weapon that it has been known to accidentally discharge if dropped?" Mike looks up to see John shake his head. "Well, it can. Hasn't happened enough yet to trigger a recall but it has happened. You need to do two things, ok? First, keep the safety on, second, keep the chamber empty," Mike says, pulling the pump back part way to discharge the round, then flipping on the safety. "Go to the range and practice so you become proficient at picking up, flipping off the safety, then pumping the action." He hands the shotgun to John. "Listen, I need

to report back to the county office that we made the inspection. Normally I would need to report the findings of the visit, but as long as you can do what I ask, and get a locker to put this in, I'll fudge the report a bit. That way you will avoid a law enforcement officer visit and fine, ok?"

"Shit," John says, "they can do that? In my own home? I can't believe the damn cops can come into my own home and tell me what to do. It's their fault for not keeping the streets safe that made me buy this in the first place." John's voice rises at the mention of police involvement. He seems irritated, borderline angry.

"When it comes to firearm safety and awareness, they sure can. Are we good here? Will you do this?" Mike asks. He's a little concerned at John's change of tone, especially while holding a firearm, but maybe he just had a bad run-in with a police officer at some point.

"Yes. Yes, of course," John replies.

He opens the garage door, still holding the shotgun. "I'll see you out this way," he says.

Hitting the garage door opener, he walks Mike to the front of the opening. "Thanks for stopping by. I appreciate it," he says.

They shake hands and Mike heads back to the truck. Just before he reaches the back of the ambulance and crosses out of John's sight he looks back. John Cray is just standing there, watching him. Mike can't quite place the look on his face or in his eyes, but suddenly John Cray looks a little too serious, perhaps still angry at the thought of police coming into his home.

Mike reaches for the door handle...

...and opened his eyes to his living room.

Getting up, he headed into his own kitchen for a drink of water before going back to bed. *Well, I did all I could do,* he thought.

He walked down the hallway to his bedroom as quietly as possible, so as not to awaken Sal. Entering his room he felt his way through the darkness to his side of the bed and crawled in. He didn't hear Sally's deep breathing anymore, and reaching over, he found her side of the bed empty. *Must be in the bathroom*, he thought, getting his pillow firmed up underneath his head. He was facing her direction, so he'd know when she came back to bed. Gently, he drifted off to sleep.

. . . .

The next morning Mike opened his eyes. He felt rested even though he hadn't gotten to sleep until after the blink and John Cray encounter. The empty other side of his bed greeted him. *She's up early as usual*, he thought. Rolling over, he looked at the clock and saw that it was 8:30 a.m. *Shit, I'm going to be late for work.*

Getting up, he headed to the bathroom for the morning ritual, then to the kitchen.

"Sal, why didn't you wake me earlier?" he asked.

Sally didn't answer. He looked around, wondering where she was. "Sal?" he called out.

Still no answer.

Mike quickly checked the other rooms of the house – the game room, spare room, back porch, and then opened Reese's door. There Mike paused, confused.

Reese's room was that of a typical college kid, with rock band posters on the walls, a desk littered with school books, notebooks, and a desktop computer, and a CD rack with the latest in pop, rap and rock music. Or, at least it used to be. The large desk had been replaced with a much smaller one. On top of the desk crayons and legos awaited in their boxes and bins next to a stack of coloring books and comics. The rock posters were gone, replaced with posters of Star Wars and Disney characters.

What the hell? Mike wondered. *What happened to Reese's room? I mean, it's still his room, but from like, ten years ago when he was still a kid.*

Heading back through the house, Mike went into the garage. His car was there, but Sally's was gone. "Maybe at the store," he muttered.

Back in the bedroom, he picked up his mobile phone and dialed her number from memory.

After several rings, he heard "Hello?" It was her voice, but it sounded different, as if she was hesitant to answer the call.

"Sal, where are you, hun?" Mike asked.

A long silence. "I'm at my home, Mike," she answered. "Why are you calling, are you ok?"

"Honey, *I'm* home. I just got up and you are definitely not here," Mike replied, a hint of confusion in his voice.

Another silence. "Mike, are you ok? You know I don't live with you anymore. I had to move on."

"What?" Mike exclaimed. "Since when? You were here last night, sleeping."

"Mike, I think you might be having another episode. You need to call your doctor." A brief pause. "We've been divorced for over five years now. I just couldn't do it anymore. Your PTSD, the stress, that was one thing, but I just couldn't deal with it after Reese was killed. You know that," she said softly.

Mike was stunned. A painful ache began to grow in the pit of his stomach. He sat down in the armchair; the same one he was in last night.

"What do you mean, Reese was killed?" he asked shakily. "He was just here this weekend, with us."

Sally paused again. "Mike, you need to call Dr. Birachi. I think you are in denial again. Reese has been gone for ten years now. That man with the shotgun...I still can't believe he did that at a school, Mike." Now Sally's voice was shaking. "Mike, I can't do this again. Give your doc a call, ok? I care about you but I can't think about this right now."

The phone clicked into silence.

Mike was stunned. He sat in his living room, not sure what to think or do. How could Reese be gone? He and Sally divorced? They were both just here. And what was this about some shooting at a school, at

Reese's school? *This can't be true.*

Getting up, Mike went into the office just off the front hallway, and looked at the wall-to-wall bookcase. He spied what he wanted – the family vacation photo album.

Dropping it on the desk he began to flip through it, starting at the back. *We were at Lake Tahoe last summer, right before Reese left for college again. We had a blast at the lake. Sally took lots of photos.* Flipping through the back of the book, he saw nothing but blank pages.

Before that should have been the photos of Reese's high school graduation, first car, prom night, football games... But the blank pages continued to flip by as Mike turned them faster and faster.

Suddenly he stopped turning the pages. He was looking at a photo of Sally and Reese, who looked to be about eleven. It was taken at a school cafeteria; he can see the Bobcat banners hanging on the wall in the background. The Bobcats were the middle school football team Reese played on.

You mean to tell me the last photo in our family album is of Reese and Sally at middle school? he thought.

Then the tears came, the wracking sobs of a man who had just learned his only son had died, been murdered, in fact. All the memories he had after that were still there, but the evidence was also clearly in front of him that Reese had been gone for a decade.

What was it that Sally had said about a shooting? Would Birachi have more information about that? Or, should he call Stevens at the county headquarters? Would Stevens help him? The doc was probably the best bet at this point, especially with his state of mind.

Mike didn't remember Birachi's number offhand, especially in light of the current situation; he could hardly think straight. Walking around to the other side of the office desk, he began pulling open drawers, hoping to find a business card or phone directory.

In the second drawer, he spied an aged, yellow newspaper, the Fort Bend Times. The top story headline caught his eye immediately.

Picking up the paper, Mike fell back into the office chair and began reading.

SHOOTING AT LOCAL SCHOOL
April 5th

A shooting has occurred at local area Parker Middle School, leaving five dead, including the gunman. John Cray, a local resident of the Pheasant Creek community, has been identified as the shooter in this tragic incident. It is unclear why John Cray walked into the school and began opening fire with a shotgun, and police say the incident is still under investigation.

What is known is that on April 4th, John Cray parked in the teachers' parking lot and walked towards the temporary classroom buildings located adjacent to the main school. Several students were moving from one class to another and several teachers were outside to monitor the students. Cray approached a male teacher and, from a distance of approximately ten feet, opened fire, killing the teacher and striking several students. Cray fired several rounds before the school police officer was able to fire upon and kill him. In addition to the teacher, who's name is being withheld pending notification of his family, three students were killed.

Our sources speculate that Cray may have suspected his wife of having an affair with the murdered teacher and that the children involved were simply innocent bystanders.

• • • •

Mike dropped the paper on the desk and stared at it.

I did this. It was Cray who pulled the trigger, but I did this. This is what Birachi was talking about, the butterfly effect; the unintended consequences. Or perhaps it is fate, setting things back to whatever balance the universe needs. After all, Cray died in a shooting, just not by his own hand. Perhaps it is a vengeful god, punishing me for playing, well, playing God.

Suddenly he had a thought. *Be it a vengeful god or fate, I can fix this. I can go back and change the past again. Maybe all I have to do is not go see him in advance of his accident.*

Looking down, he saw the scar on his hand. *But this didn't go away when I changed the future for Joey. It still happened, just in a different way.*

I'll fix it. No matter what, I'll fix it.

Chapter Eight

H ey, Frank, going to make a quick stop if that's ok with you," Mike says. He knows the Cray family lives off of Six, just up ahead in the Pheasant Creek neighborhood.

"Sure. Where to?" Frank asks.

Mike has just blinked back to this moment in time. He realizes he has just set things in motion that will lead to a fatal shooting of several people, including his son, unless he can somehow change it, stop it from happening.

They are driving on Highway Six after leaving the no-injury accident.

"Just to that gas station over there," Mike says. "I have to piss like crazy."

Mike pulls into the gas station and parks near the air and water equipment. "Be just a second," he says, jumping out.

He goes into the bathroom, not really needing to urinate, but needing a moment to think this through. Stopping at the sink, he begins to slowly wash his hands.

Ok, crisis averted, *he thinks.* We go back to the station and wait for Klutzy Cray to have his little accident later this evening. I wonder how long I can stay in this blink? Can I stay long enough to work the call again? Will I try a little less hard this time, knowing the guy could end up being a mass murderer, a killer of children, including my own son?

Mike looks up at the mirror. His eyes look hollow and stare back at him blankly. You know you can't do that, *he tells himself.* You're a medic. The goal hasn't changed; you try to save lives. You just want to change the outcome of the future, not the present.

Mike finishes up and they head back to the station.

Later that day the alert tones ring for another car accident. This one is a little more serious, and they transport a middle-aged woman to the hospital as a precaution with low back pain. Her vital signs were stable, as were her neurological signs; she could move all her fingers and toes, but it's best to be safe. So after getting her strapped to a backboard and with a cervical collar in place, they take an uneventful trip to the emergency room.

Back at the station, Mike watches the clock.

Frank cooks dinner, pasta with a homemade tomato sauce. They eat while Mike keeps an eye on the clock.

The late evening news is on, and Mike stops watching the clock. The time has passed and no calls have come in. Something is wrong, *he thinks.*

"Time to hit the sack for me," Frank says. "You can keep watching the clock if you want. Yeah, I noticed. Watch it all you want, but you can't change time, it just keeps marching on."

That causes Mike to look up suddenly, and then... blink...

Mike opened his eyes to see he had returned to his home office. The faded newspaper headline still stared back at him from the top of the desk where he'd left it earlier that day. His wife was still gone, his son still dead.

"What the hell?" he cried out loud. "That should have changed it; I didn't go see the bastard!" He then looked at the scar on his hand. "But you are still here, to remind me I can't always change things, aren't you?"

Mike began to think. *There* has *to be a way around this. It just may take more drastic measures.*

Hey, Frank, going to make a quick stop if that's ok with you," Mike says. He knows the Cray family lives off of Six, just up ahead in the Pheasant Creek neighborhood.

"Sure. Where to?" Frank asks.

I don't think I can bullshit my way out of it this time. But can I trust him, I mean fully trust Frank with this? Even though he is dead and buried, could letting him in on my little secret somehow alter things in an even worse way?

"I just need to stop and see this guy I know," Mike says. "He lives right up here in the Pheasant Creek subdivision. He, um, owes me something."

"Oh yeah, what's that?" Frank asks.

My kid's life, *Mike thinks.* "Look, Frank, I need to trust you with something, ok? We've been partners for quite a while, and friends even longer. You are like a brother to me, man. Can I trust you?"

"*Of course, Mike, with anything. I swear on my life.*"

Oh don't do that, *Mike thinks,* It doesn't end well for you, my friend.

"*Listen, this guy I need to see. It's something personal, and I need to keep it quiet. Hopefully things will go ok, but I need you to wait at the truck, and back me up if something happens. Ok?*"

"*Sure, man. Whatever you say. Does this have something to do with Sally? I know you guys are tight, but all these long shifts, well I know how sometimes lovers can stray...*" he says.

Mike jumps on that. He gives Frank a quick glance as he pulls onto Sugar Way and then nods slowly. Frank thinks Sal is cheating on me. Let him think that. It's far easier to believe than the truth. Ironic how a fidelity issue could have been what set off Cray against that teacher, and now I'm going to see him for allegedly the same thing.

"*Aw man, that sucks. I'm sorry,*" Frank says softly.

"*Just wait in the truck. And remember, back me up, ok?*"

Frank nods as Mike climbs out.

Mike goes to the door, again. He rings the doorbell, again.

John Cray opens the door, just that crack. Suspicious bastard, *Mike thinks.* Something *was* off with this guy even back then (or now).

"*Can I help you?*" John Cray asks.

"*Yes. My name is Mike Spence and I work with the county ambulance service. You may not know this, but whenever a resident purchases a firearm, we get notified and are asked to stop by and do a safety check. Do you mind if I come in, Mr. Cray?*"

John looks at him sideways, narrowing his eyes. "*Never heard of that before. But this is my first purchase so I guess I wouldn't have, huh?*"

John steps to the side of the door. "*Come on in,*" he says. *John extends his hand and shakes Mike's as he enters, then closes the door. He notices*

*that the uniformed man is wearing medical gloves. "I hope those are clean,"
John jokes.*

*Mike had put on the gloves before ringing the doorbell, grabbing them
out of the small pouch he wears around his belt. "Sorry, occupational
hazard, I guess."*

*Walking into the living room with the big man, Mike asks, "Anyone
else at home with you, Mr. Cray?"*

"Nope. Kids are both at school, wife's at work," John replies.

*John takes Mike through the living room, kitchen, and into a small
laundry area. Mike recognizes the laundry area, having seen it now from
both the garage and the kitchen entry.*

"I bought it for home security, you know," John is saying.

*"Can't be too careful, I know," Mike says. "We want to make sure
things are buttoned up though, so that we don't have to pay an unnecessary
visit. Lot of accidents happen with firearms, especially with new owners.
Although I'm sure you are very careful."*

*"I sure am," John replies. "Since I just got it, I haven't had a chance to
get a storage locker yet, so I'm keeping it in here up high, away from my
kids. I got all the safety bases covered that way."*

So you think, Mike says to himself. You don't know what's coming.

John stops and begins to reach up for the Remington.

*"Hold up," Mike says suddenly. "Do you mind if I get it? I'm a bit
particular about these sorts of things."*

"Be my guest," John says. "But be careful, it's loaded."

*Mike steps past John and looks up at the overhead shelf. He can just see
the barrel sticking past the edge of the shelf. It's a bit high for Mike, and
he doesn't want to reach up blindly. "Listen, do you have a step ladder I
could use?"*

*"Sure, it's in the garage. Let me get it." Cray opens the door behind
him leading to the garage, steps out briefly, and returns with a two-step
ladder, setting it up for Mike.*

"Thanks," Mike says.

Mike steps up on the ladder so he can be eye level with the shelf. Now he can see the gleaming black barrel of the shotgun, and using both hands, reaches out and gently picks it up, pulls it to his chest, and steps back to ground level.

"Remington, pump action. Nice one," Mike says. "I love the scrollwork on the barrel, and the wooden stock is a nice deep brown color. You said it's loaded. Is there a round in the chamber?"

"Damn straight there is. I want to be able to grab and shoot, you know?"

"I can understand that. Looks like the safety is off as well. Listen, did they mention when you purchased this weapon that it has been known to accidentally discharge if dropped?" Mike looks up to see John shake his head. "Well, it can."

Mike pauses for a moment, staring at the weapon in his gloved hands. In one version of reality, Cray dies and four people benefit from his organs. In another, Cray lives and four other people die, including Mike's son. Is there a reason for that? Some sort of even exchange on the big board of life? Or is it merely a coincidence? He can almost imagine an agent of God bartering with Old Man Death: "I'll trade you four organ transplant survivors for four others in a mass shooting; what do ya say? I'll even throw in the shooter as a bonus as the boss can be vengeful on occasion, and after all, He gets them all in the end."

Mike pushes the barrel of the shotgun up under John's chin and pulls the trigger.

The blast is loud in the small space, but Mike is hoping it doesn't carry too far outside the exterior walls of the home. Hopefully anyone hearing it, including Frank, will think it's a car backfiring a block over.

The round takes John in the fleshy part of the chin, and Mike watches as the back of his head explodes, leaving a spray of red and gray on the wall across from the washer and dryer. Not quite in the original spot, but close enough. John falls to the floor with a thump.

Mike then takes the weapon, raises it above his head, and while ensuring it is pointed away from him just in case, he drops it butt first to the ground. The shotgun bounces with a large crack and then falls across John's dying body.

Mike looks down to see that none of the splatter has hit him; his uniform is clean. But he is trapped between John and the kitchen entry, blood already pooling around John's head. Can't exit that way, *he thinks.* Can't risk contaminating the scene.

Grabbing the step-ladder, Mike opens the door leading out into the garage, and places it next to the wall. He then triggers the garage door opener. Once the door has stopped its movement upwards, Mike depresses the button again and quickly moves towards the closing door. With the door about five feet up and coming down slowly, he takes a large step to avoid the photo eye that would trigger the door to reverse while simultaneously ducking to avoid the lower edge of it. Successfully navigating this, he walks calmly but quickly to the truck, striping his gloves and putting them in his pocket as he moves.

As he enters the truck, Frank asks, "Did you hear that?"

"Hear what?" Mike asks, shaking his head no, and putting the truck in gear.

"It was a faint pop noise, like a car backfiring."

"I didn't hear it in the house," Mike replied. "That must have been what it was."

Mike slowly drives off and heads back to the station to await the inevitable call when Cray's wife arrives home later in the afternoon.

If the timing is right, *Mike muses,* we will be on that car crash when he gets found and another unit will respond. That will prevent any unnecessary questions from Frank as to why we were at a house earlier today where the owner ended up dead.

Mike. Time for breakfast," Sal called from the other room.

Mike, in the office, sat still for a moment, a look of relief on his face. The newspaper was gone from the surface of the desk, and Sally was in the kitchen. He could smell the eggs that she'd fried.

Getting up, he went to the kitchen and gave her a bear hug, hiding the tears welling up in his eyes.

"What's that for?" she asked.

"I just love you, that's all."

Pulling back, she stared up at him. "Mike, are you ok? You look like you've seen a ghost or something."

"Reese...where is he?" Mike asked slowly. He needed to know, but was worried that somehow he would still be dead, regardless of the horrible thing that Mike had done during the blink.

"He's at school, of course. Got an A on his semester test in math," Sally said with a smile. "I just spoke to him yesterday."

At that, Mike's legs gave out. Sally held him up and helped him to the kitchen table.

"Mike! What's wrong?" she cried.

"Nothing, hun. As long as he is ok, nothing at all."

Chapter Nine

It had been a few days in his head since "the killing," as Mike had come to think of it, although it had happened decades ago in reality. His hands shook when he thought about it; it was still too raw an experience. His heart wanted to feel guilt for what he had done, but his head was able to rationalize it.

After all, what exactly had he done? Just what fate originally had in store for John Cray. The tragic accident of John Cray had simply happened by a different hand, but by the same mechanism, the same bullet crashing through his brain, the same location; all the same. All the little dominos that John had stacked against his life had still happened prior to Mike's intervention: he purchased the gun, he left it loaded, he put it on a high shelf; this time Mike had just provided the nudge that brought the dominos crashing down.

More importantly, Reese was safe. He had undone what he had unintentionally done. On one hand, it was no different than an accident being prevented. No one intends to get killed in a car crash, or to slip and fall in the bathroom and break their neck, but it happens. By taking some reasonable steps, you sometimes can prevent those accidents, not always, but sometimes. So Mike had just taken a reasonable step to prevent an unstable person from taking the lives of several kids and a teacher. He could live with that.

What Mike was really starting to consider was that perhaps this altering of the past leading to a negative outcome was in the minority; after all, not everyone is a mass murderer like Cray. Most people are just normal people going about their normal lives. So Mike going back in time through his blinks and nudging things for a different outcome would surely have a more positive outcome than what originally happened to those people, and in the majority of cases there wouldn't be a John Cray scenario. Most would be like Joey Vasquez and have a happy ending; at least in theory.

Having justified the killing in his mind, at least for the moment, Mike resolved himself to try again. He had just the one he wanted to fix – the one that had haunted him the most all those years, the one that led to the current situation of his increased blinks, his inability to sleep, his survivors guilt, and all the rest.

He wanted to go back to the night Frank died and save him from that fateful bullet.

. . . .

Mike was back at the cemetery. He had decided it was time for one last visit with Frank before he blinked. He wanted to talk it through one more time as well; remove any lingering doubts about what he would attempt.

Why would he doubt this? Frank didn't deserve to die any more than Joey did. What scared him, the reason for his doubt, was not knowing what it would do to Mike's own life if Frank survived. Would he stay in emergency medicine, continuing to work on the ambulance with him? Would the continuous, long shifts, sleepless nights, and day after day of trauma and tragedy take even more of a toll on Mike than his current condition of PTSD?

Could that road lead to Sal divorcing him, like had happened with so many others in public service? The spouse at home worrying day after day if their loved one will make it home from the next call; that takes its own toll, causes its own form of PTSD, doesn't it? It's not an easy life, being married to a first responder. They spend those twenty-four hour shifts alone, wondering and worrying. They take care of the home and the kids, having to act like a single parent for those days.

Maybe Frank surviving would lead to something better. Mike's mind will be more at ease, no more guilt for being the guy that survived that night. It all hinged on Frank being the first one to the door; that could just as easily have been him. At this thought, he absently reached up and rubbed that spot on his chest, the one that hurt for no reason on occasion. The doc said it was psychosomatic, his mind's ways of dealing with the fact that his partner got shot by creating a phantom pain in the same spot the bullet entered Frank's body; similar to an amputee still feeling their fingers even though the arm is gone.

Mike stooped, placing the required flowers on Frank's headstone.

He didn't have much to say, as he wanted to say it all once Frank was back; all twenty years' worth of missed conversations. But he felt it was important to come to this place. Hopefully for the last time.

Suddenly, Mike had a thought. "I remember this one time, Frank, when we were at the station, and I guess I was riding the clock a little too much, and you made an offhand comment about 'watching the clock all I wanted, but time just marched on'. Well, I've found that time *does* march on, you can't stop that, but you can alter its path slightly, and with huge outcomes. I'm going to do that for you, Frank. I'm going to give time a little nudge and hope for a vastly different outcome.

"See you soon, Frank."

• • • •

Mike pulls up to the curb in front of the red brick house. A single light filters out behind blinds in what is probably the bedroom. After putting the ambulance in park, he grabs the mic, hanging on the clip from the dash, and calls dispatch.

"Medic Three on scene" he says, and replaces the mic on its hook.

"Looks like we beat the fire department again," Frank says with a chuckle, "due to your lead foot driving."

Mike smiles at that. He remembers this part of the conversation fondly. Frank and Mike were always teasing each other about the other's driving habits, although both were ultra-safe drivers, having seen the consequences of unsafe driving up close and personal all too often.

Frank starts to step out but Mike grabs his arm. "Let's be careful tonight," he says.

Frank looks back. "Always, man."

Both Mike and Frank step out of the cab and grab their respective gear from compartments on either side of the ambulance. Frank is closest to the house and as he walks towards the door, shouldering the respiratory pack, Mike steps it up to get beside him, carrying the cardiac monitor and patient clipboard.

This is it, Mike thinks, Just like before. The front door is centered on the walkway with large bushes to either side of the small porch. The single overhead light illuminates the wooden exterior, and Mike can see the faded and peeling paint. He can also see the door slightly ajar, darkness beyond. This view was blocked before, as he approached from behind Frank. Now, walking side by side, he reaches out with his right arm, touching Frank on the shoulder.

Frank looks over at Mike, having also seen the cracked doorway. He shrugs briefly, then turns back and begins to take that last fatal step forward to knock on the door, which in turn will open it wider into the barrel of the waiting 9mm.

Suddenly Mike, his hand still on Frank's shoulder, gives a hard shove, pushing Frank to the right off of the sidewalk and into the grass in front of the large bush flanking the door.

Mike underestimates the force he had to use to push Frank. In doing so, he inadvertently steps to the right, filling the void that Frank was just in.

A sudden flash of light drives back the darkness. Mike feels a burning in his chest, like a hot poker from a fireplace has just been shoved inside him.

He falls backwards onto the sidewalk, pivoting from the push against his chest, landing at an angle with his head bouncing off the grass. Although the back of his head hurts from the tap on the ground, it is nothing like the pain in his chest.

He's having trouble breathing. This must be what COPD feels like, he thinks. He is able to breathe in but he is having trouble getting the breath back out again.

Faintly, he hears Frank, "Medic Three, we have a man down! Shots fired!"

Mike senses something to his left, a presence of some sort. Rotating his head in that direction, he sees a man on the walkway between where he fell and the ambulance. Only, it is not a man, although it has a man's shape. Mike can see the ambulance faintly through the shape. It is there but not fully there. Like the transporter on Star Trek when Captain Kirk is partially gone on his next adventure. This man's shape is tall, very tall. It must be seven feet at least, Mike thinks. It's wearing a tuxedo of some sort, but it looks ancient, like something you would see from the early 1800's – faded black and tattered around the edges. It's hands appear huge, like they could grasp your head in one and pick you up with no effort, and the fingers are elongated. The fingernails are even longer, and sharp.

Mike's eyes move upward to the creature's face. It is ancient, the skin wrinkled with deep crevices, the lips cracked with age, and the nose crooked, shifting a little to the left. The eyes, however, are fiery black, the deepest black one has ever imagined but with a red glow burning beneath, like a view into hell itself.

It's Old Man Death, Mike thinks. I've always imagined death as an opponent trying to steal away lives while I worked to save them as a paramedic. Is this what people see when they are dying, like I am dying now? *Old Man Death stares back at him and smiles a horrible, sharp-toothed smile.*

Mike is able to turn his head to the right and sees Frank still over by the bushes, radio in hand. He is crouched down, staying out of the field of fire from the doorway.

They make eye contact and Frank looks upset, but also kinda angry. Why would he be angry?

"Damn it, Mike," Frank says from his cover, "it's not supposed to go down this way, man. Don't worry, I can fix this."

Mike's breathing has become more difficult. He's not sure what Frank is talking about. He doesn't think this can be fixed in time. The goal was to avoid the shot, which was why he pushed Frank out of the way. Just damn bad luck that he lost his balance. His last coherent thought before dying was at least I saved Frank.

Then, nothing.

Chapter Ten

Darkness. Nothingness. The sleep of the dead.

Suddenly, there is movement, pressure on the chest, a gentle shaking. Now the shaking and pressure become more firm. Mike opens his eyes in the darkness to see Frank standing there.

"Get up," Frank says.

Turning his head, Mike glances at the clock on the nightstand, the only form of illumination in the room. The digital clock's blue numbers show it is 2:30 a.m.

"Did I sleep through the tones?" Mike asks sleepily.

"Just get up," Frank repeats, walking out of the bedroom.

Mike throws his legs out of bed, sits for a moment shaking out the cobwebs, and stands up. He is in his work pants, his blue EMS tee, and socks. He always sleeps partially dressed to allow himself to get out of the station faster when the alert tones go off. He can go from sound asleep to fully awake in just under ninety seconds.

Heading into the hallway and into the small living quarters, he finds Frank perched on the edge of the sofa. Mike takes the single chair across from him.

Frank just stares at him for a moment.

"Do you remember?" Frank asks.

"Remember what?"

"The shooting, Mike. Do you remember the shooting?"

"Which one?" Mike replies, the cobwebs still in his head. "We've had so many."

Frank pauses and stares at him. It makes Mike feel slightly uncomfortable, as if he won't like the response he is waiting to hear.

"Mine. Yours," Frank responds.

Mike just stares back for a moment. He is unsure of what Frank is talking about, but he begins to feel a nagging ache in his chest, and he reaches up to touch it.

"*Come on, Mike, we don't have much time,*" *Frank says urgently, looking up to the clock on the wall above the television. "I need you to remember.*"

Mike rubs the spot on his chest. Then it comes flooding back to him. Frank being shot, the blinks, and his finding a way to go back into the flashbacks and fix things.

He remembers going back to the night Frank was killed and trying to fix it.

He remembers taking the bullet and Frank saying 'Don't worry, I can fix this.'

He remembers staring at the face of Old Man Death, an imaginary adversary who is apparently more real than he thought.

He remembers dying. But if I died instead of Frank, how can we be here? *Mike thinks.*

Looking up at Frank, his eyes widening, he suddenly realizes the truth. "You brought us back here, didn't you?" he asks, quietly. "You have blinked back to this moment, not me, 'cause I died."

Frank just stares for a moment, then nods. "Tell me what you remember," he says, "but be quick, time is moving forward."

Mike briefly tells Frank that he remembers the original call, Frank dying at the hands of the old man with dementia. How Mike discovered he could go back and adjust the incidents they experienced, just enough to change the outcome.

"Then I went back to that night, this night I suppose, and I saved you, but in the process, I ended up getting shot instead," Mike finishes.

"That all happened," Frank says slowly, "but that call, the one where I died, that was not the original call. He looks down to the floor and then back at Mike. "During the original call, you *were killed. It actually happened to you* first.

"You were up for the call so you were riding shotgun. We got to the house and you went in first, as usual. We didn't expect anything; hell, it was just a medical call, remember? Quiet neighborhood, middle of the

night. When we got to the door and saw it open we should have waited, backed off and called for police assistance. But we didn't. It was late, we were both tired from too many calls earlier in the shift, and we wanted to get in and get done.

"You pushed the door open and the old guy fired one shot. You took it right in the chest and died within two minutes as it ripped open your left ventricle. You bled out internally.

"The old man dropped his weapon and came out of the house afterwards. He didn't realize what he had done at first, but the noise of the shot brought him around to reality, so he came out to see if he could help. But it was too late."

"Wait," Mike says. "You mean I died? But, I don't remember that at all. What I do remember is getting out of EMS. I have a job at the insurance agency. My kid, Reese, is in college. Sal and I have a good marriage. That is what happened."

Frank shakes his head. "Just like Joey didn't remember dying, you don't either."

"How do you know about that?" Mike asks.

"I was there, remember? But I'll get to that in a minute, if we have time.

"The fact of the matter, the honest truth, was that you died first. I lived. I lived with the survivors' guilt. My life fell apart afterwards. I couldn't function. I lost my job first, then my home.

"I found myself on the street drowning in a bottle of booze, whenever I had enough to buy one. That wasn't too hard, actually, most folks will drop a dollar or two for a homeless guy with a cardboard sign.

"One day, I was sitting by the side of the road, sign in hand, working the intersection, and this little car beeps its horn at me. I go over to the window as it rolls down, and it's Sally. She was going to hand me a few dollars as she would any other street person, but then we recognized each other.

"I was embarrassed for her to see me like that, but she pulled over in a

nearby parking lot and called me over out of the street so we could talk.

"She ended up buying me a meal and saving my life, which in turn, saved yours. Sally told me things had been rough for her after you died. The small savings and life insurance you had didn't go very far. She struggled from job to job, was barely able to get by on her own, but couldn't see a path to another relationship or getting re-married, even if that would have been the best thing for Reese. So she existed, she just tried to go from moment to moment. She was ruined, Mike."

"Reese," Mike says hesitantly. "What about Reese?"

Frank answers. "He suffered from not having a father figure in his life. He was always getting into trouble at school; fights, drugs, that sort of thing. He ended up dropping out of high school and got in with the wrong crowd.

"She told me he was currently serving ten years on a felony drug charge up at Huntsville Prison."

Mike is stunned by what he is hearing. He always thought they would be ok if something happened to him. Sally was such a strong person; he was sure she would bounce back. But from what Frank was telling him, that never happened, to either her or his son.

"She was able to help me, though. At that moment, she was working at a church that provided assistance for the homeless. Mainly a hot meal and an opportunity for them to preach the gospel but also some assistance in the form of performing some jobs for the church or its members. Menial labor usually, but you were paid out of the church donations. The only catch was you had to get in a twelve-step program and stay sober, which I did.

"Once I was sober I started having these dreams, or so I thought of them at first. I was dreaming of our EMS days together, Mike. Every night I would go to sleep and have these vivid dreams about the calls we had gone on, man, down to the last detail.

"During one such dream, I remembered how things had gone bad on this call. There was this guy, he was pinned in his car after a head-on accident, and it took the fire department too long to get him out; I mean

they did everything they could, but his leg was pinned under the dashboard and it just took too damn long. He ended up dying right there in front of us.

"I remembered this in the dream, and when the fire department arrived, I said, 'I'm going to put a tourniquet on his leg, and I need you to cut off his ankle where he is pinned with the Jaws of Life.' They looked at me like I was crazy but I took full responsibility for the call and ordered them to do it.

"We got the guy out and he lived. There was a hearing with the State Health Board but it was determined that if normal procedures had been followed he would have died.

"It was then that I realized I could change the past. But I had no control over which dreams I was going to have, unless I really thought about a particular incident before I fell asleep. Then, I found I was able to dream about that *incident.*

"I saw how horrible my life turned out, and how bad it had been for Sally and Reese, and thought if I could change places with you I would. I knew you would live a much better life, and do so much to protect your family, and they would thrive and prosper with you in their lives.

"The choice was easy for me, really.

"So, one night, I thought long and hard about the call where you died, when that old man shot you, and I went there."

Frank paused for a moment, then continued. "At first, I tried to prevent the shooting altogether. But nothing I tried seemed to work. The first time, I tried holding you back and waiting for the fire department. That time, the guy was in his living room, gun hidden beside him on the sofa. We went in and I thought since he didn't fire at the doorway all was good. He pulled out the pistol and shot you at point blank range.

"Another time, I tried having us approach the house from the rear after we noticed the front door opened. That time, he shot you through the kitchen window. I even tried not going to the call, but we kept ending up back there, and you kept getting shot."

Mike quietly asks, "How many times did you try?"

Frank hesitates before answering. "I tried eight times, and each time you still ended up dead. I realized something then with this madness I was in. Some things couldn't be changed. That for some reason, be it fate or an angry god, that a sacrifice was required, a death had to happen. We were not going to get out of this without one of us taking that bullet."

Nodding to the scar on Mike's hand, he said, "Kind of like that scar there. The way it happened changed, but it still happened right?"

"So, on the ninth time, I didn't try to save us both, I only tried to save you. When the alert tones went off, as they will go off in a few minutes, we got up, and I offered to take the call, so I would be first in. And by going first in, I got to the door first and took that bullet, and died."

"But how can you be here now and telling me all this if you died?" Mike asks.

"Because you went back and changed it, and this time it was you who took the bullet; again. Mike, you have to let this one play out and let me die. You have to move on from the guilt you feel about me and live your life with Sal and Reese. I know it's been hard, but you have to, for your sake as well as theirs.

"Where I'm at, it's not bad. I'm really not allowed to talk about it, and it is not what most people think, but I'm ok. You don't have to worry about me anymore, ok?"

"Frank, when I died, I saw, well, someone or something else was there with us. It was back behind us towards the truck. Did you see it?" Mike asks.

"Yeah Mike, I did. I also saw him when I died, as well as a few times since. You want to avoid that one if you can; he plays for keeps."

Then Frank smiles at him. "You asked how I knew about Joey. We only have a few minutes left before the tones go off, but I have time to answer that.

"I know about Joey because every time you go back into one of your blinks, your flashbacks, I'm actually there. I relive it just as you relive it.

That's one of the magical things about the place where I am. Whenever you relive a memory of me, whether it is in a blink, or just thinking about me, or anyone that has died as a matter of fact, we are there. We exist.

"It really is true that people live on in your memories of them. We shared so much time and so much of life together, sometimes giving others life, sometimes comforting them in their death, that I am able to share those experiences with you whenever you have them.

"So don't be sad that I'm gone, because I'm still here, where I am supposed to be.

"But you have been given a special gift; one that allows you to go back and fix some of the mistakes that others made, fix some of the tragic accidents that didn't need to occur. Some of those may end badly anyway, such as mine, but most will be permitted to have a do-over. Some you won't be able to correct, but others you will.

"Go back and use that gift for them, for the ones we couldn't save. And remember I will be there, and I'll guide you as I can, but usually I'm not allowed to offer much in the way of help; you will be driving destiny, not I."

Mike has started crying. He can't believe what he has heard from Frank. That these memories and blinks are not only a way to change the past, but a way to connect back with him. Most importantly, that he has been saved from a tragic fate of his own, one that led to dire consequences for his family beyond anything he could imagine. He has been given a gift, not only of his own life, but maybe a way to continue to help others, and to get past the PTSD that has haunted him for so long. A way to heal while helping others, albeit in the past.

"Frank, are you sure there's not a way out of this for you, too?" he asks.

"I'm sure, Mike."

The sirens suddenly go off over the station PA system. The dispatcher's voice comes over the radio. "Medic Three, medical call," they hear.

"Let's go," Frank says.

He feels the grass under him. Warm sunlight on his face. Slowly,

Mike opens his eyes to look out across the quiet, empty cemetery. He sits up, realizing he has been laying on top of Frank's grave. A tear slowly rolls down his cheek as he thinks back on all that has occurred; not just in the past few moments of the blink, but of all the moments in his life since Frank died. Mike realizes that his life is a gift, one bought with the most precious commodity of all.

Determined to make the most of that gift, he gets up and heads home.

· · · ·

Hey Sal," Mike says softly upon arriving home later that evening. She's groggy for only a moment, and then sits straight up on the couch where she had been dozing. "Mike, where have you been? I've been worried sick about you."

"I'm sorry, hun. I had to go visit Frank. Spur of the moment thing."

"Are you ok?" she asks.

Mike thinks for a moment before answering. "Yes. Yes I am. I know I haven't been for a while, but I'm truly ok now."

"Are you still having blinks?"

"I think I will always have them, hun. But I think I've found a way to control them and make them a little less painful when they occur," Mike says softly, smiling.

Sally smiles back at him and they embrace.

Mike is sitting in his favorite chair. He has been thinking about that call with the two-year old. Her and her momma were coming out of the grocery store and momma didn't have a good hand on her little girl. The driver didn't see her dart out in front of his big sedan until it was too late.

This one just needs a little nudge, Mike thinks. *Maybe I can be beside them and remind mom to grab her little girl's hand, or maybe I can be in front and grab her when she runs towards the car. Either way, it should just take a little nudge to prevent her from getting run over.*

He wonders for a moment if he will see that tall man again, the one with the haggard face. Old Man Death. He knows he will see him at his own eventual demise, but wonders if he will appear and try to stop Mike from nudging the dominos in a different direction. Mike wonders what he will do if that happens, but decides to save that worry for another day.

Mike leans back in the chair, getting himself ready. He'll save the child first, then give Frank a hug and tell him everything is ok.

Mike closes his eyes, then...

Blink.

Don't miss out!

Visit the website below and you can sign up to receive emails whenever Tim Laseter publishes a new book. There's no charge and no obligation.

https://books2read.com/r/B-A-FHPT-YFZZB

BOOKS2READ

Connecting independent readers to independent writers.

About the Author

Tim Laseter is a veteran and former paramedic who spent six years running 911 calls in Texas, and his experiences form the basis for his fictional tale, *Blink*. He is currently working on a series of dark stories set in theme parks, where he worked for over three decades. *A Ghost on the Cliff* is the first release of Tim's Dark Corners Collection. Tim Laseter resides in Texas with his spouse and cats.

Follow Tim Laseter at:

www.facebook.com/Tim.Laseter.Author

www.linkedin.com/in/timlaseter

Read more at https://tlaseter191.wixsite.com/tim-laseter-author.